SPECIAL MESSAGE TO READERS

This book is published under the auspices of

THE ULVERSCROFT FOUNDATION

(registered charity No. 264873 UK)

Established in 1972 to provide funds for research, diagnosis and treatment of eye diseases.

Examples of contributions made are: —

A Children's Assessment Unit at Moorfield's Hospital, London.

•

Twin operating theatres at the Western Ophthalmic Hospital, London.

•

A Chair of Ophthalmology at the Royal Australian College of Ophthalmologists.

•

The Ulverscroft Children's Eye Unit at the Great Ormond Street Hospital For Sick Children, London.

You can help further the work of the Foundation by making a donation or leaving a legacy. Every contribution, no matter how small, is received with gratitude. Please write for details to:

THE ULVERSCROFT FOUNDATION,
The Green, Bradgate Road, Anstey,
Leicester LE7 7FU, England.
Telephone: (0116) 236 4325

In Australia write to:

THE ULVERSCROFT FOUNDATION,
c/o The Royal Australian and New Zealand College of Ophthalmologists,
94-98 Chalmers Street, Surry Hills,
N.S.W. 2010, Australia

VICTIMS OF CIRCUMSTANCE

During the worst 'flu epidemic for fifty years, a student nurse is found dead in her room. But Golding, the forensic pathologist, believes that this wasn't as a consequence of the virulent infection . . . Under suspicion are the senior physician, revered by some and hated by others; the pathologist, from whose laboratory the poison had come; and the registrar, who gave the fatal injection . . . There is another murder before Inspector Newton tracks down the killer — and faces death in terrifying circumstances himself.

Books by Peter Conway
in the Linford Mystery Library:

MURDER IN DUPLICATE

PETER CONWAY

VICTIMS OF CIRCUMSTANCE

Complete and Unabridged

LINFORD
Leicester

First published in Great Britain by
Robert Hale Limited
London

First Linford Edition
published 2006
by arrangement with
Robert Hale Limited
London

British Library CIP Data

Conway, Peter
Victims of circumstance.—Large print ed.—
Linford mystery library
1. Murder—Investigation—Fiction
2. Physicians—Fiction 3. Detective and
mystery stories 4. Large type books
I. Title
823.9′14 [F]

ISBN 1–84617–332–9

Published by
F. A. Thorpe (Publishing)
Anstey, Leicestershire

Set by Words & Graphics Ltd.
Anstey, Leicestershire
Printed and bound in Great Britain by
T. J. International Ltd., Padstow, Cornwall

This book is printed on acid-free paper

1

Duncan Forrester, the medical registrar on duty, sighed wearily as he saw the long queue of nurses still waiting to be immunised. Everything seemed to have gone wrong for him in the preceding few days; he was desperately tired, he had just failed the MRCP examination for the third time and to cap everything, he wasn't feeling at all well. He wouldn't have been surprised if he went down with the 'flu himself; if so, he would be in good company, half the staff seemed to be off as it was.

It was typical, he thought, that the vaccine should have arrived too late to do much good. The 'flu epidemic seemed to have started in North Korea, although no one was absolutely certain about that, but one thing was clear and that was that it was the most virulent one of its kind since the great pandemic which had followed the First World War. The death rate, particularly amongst elderly people with chronic chest and heart complaints, had risen alarmingly and worse, several school children had been happily playing in the morning, only to die of acute heart failure later in the day. The popular press was having a field day, forecasting doom and even a second Black Death, while the latest in a long line of evangelists from America was drawing in audiences of thousands, urging repentance before it was too late.

'Come along, man, we haven't got all afternoon.'

Forrester whirled round and ground his teeth together as he saw the senior physician and a small group of other doctors, who had approached the trolley from the other side. He had always thought that Dr Poynter was a pompous ass and this was the last straw. The casualty department was large, but already it was beginning to look like Waterloo Station in the rush hour.

'I'm afraid you'll have to wait, sir,' he said, putting sufficient emphasis on the 'sir', just to cross the dividing line between respect and insolence. 'It'll be at least ten minutes before I'm able to finish these nurses.'

'Hmm — clearly we need a bit more organization here; there'll be another twenty of the staff along before many minutes. Sister, set up another trolley over there, will you? Hunt, you can give a hand with the injections and I'll . . . '

Forrester plunged the needle into the arm of the nurse waiting next in the queue with quite unnecessary force and pressed home the plunger. As he withdrew it and turned to throw the disposable syringe into the waste bin, picking up the next one almost in the same movement, he heard a muffled thud and saw the girl he had just injected, lying on the ground, ashen-faced.

The Home Sister clicked her tongue disapprovingly and looked towards the two girls next in line.

'You two, will you see to her please? Get her up on that couch over there — you'll have to join the end of the queue for your injections.' She glanced back over her shoulder. 'Come along, Nurse Wilkinson, you're next. Roll up your sleeve then; I can't think why you always have to be told everything twice, all the others are ready, why can't you be?'

The girl flushed, and as she came up fiddling with her cuffs, Forrester held the next syringe up to the light, expelling the last bit of air. He smiled at her reassuringly, then swabbed her arm and slid the needle smoothly in. As they got into the swing of the procedure again, he couldn't suppress a faintly malicious grin as, looking over his shoulder, he saw the chaos around the other trolley, where Poynter was waving his arms about, issuing orders in all directions. A good proportion of the senior staff now seemed to be there and as the last nurse came up, he breathed a sigh of relief and decided to leave while the going was good. Just as he was about to do so, he remembered the girl who had fainted and went across to the couch. By now, she was looking a better colour and smiled weakly up at him.

'Sorry about that,' she said, 'silly of me.'

'Not to worry, it can happen to anyone. At least we got the injection in. Feeling better now?'

'Yes, thanks.'

'Good. Why not wait there a few more minutes and then we can get someone to help you across to your room.'

He made for the door and was half-way through when he heard the familiar rasping voice cut across the room.

'Forrester!'

The registrar had had enough; he didn't even start to look round and when Poynter sent someone after him, the corridor was empty and he was nowhere to be found.

* * *

'I say, Anne, you look a bit grotty.'

'I do feel a bit funny — all weak and feeble.'

'Perhaps it's the injection, my arm's quite sore.'

'Funnily enough, mine isn't, but let's

hope it's that and not the 'flu; there are enough people off as it is.'

'Why not pop into bed?'

'I think I will.'

'Here, let me give you a hand.'

Half an hour later, Sue Kemp knocked on the door of her friend's bedroom and put her head round the door.

'How are you feeling now?'

'Not too bad, thanks.'

Despite the other girl's protests, Sue put the thermometer under her tongue and took her pulse.

'Well, at least you haven't got a fever, that's one good thing. Sure you'll be O.K.? I was going to that film at the Rialto, but I'll sit with you if you like.'

'Don't be silly Sue, I'll be all right, really. It was jolly nice of you to offer, though.'

'Sure you don't want me to tell Sister Heywood?'

'No, I'm sure it's nothing.'

'O.K. then, I'll look in again when I get back. 'Bye.'

Sue Kemp had a momentary feeling of uneasiness as she went down the corridor; it was unlike Anne to make a fuss over a little thing like a 'flu injection, but all that was forgotten a few minutes later when she met Simon in her room.

Sue Kemp had not been gone for much more than twenty minutes, when Anne Wilkinson realized that she should have asked her to send for the Home Sister. She didn't feel all right at all; what she should really have told her friend was that she had never felt worse in her whole life. It wasn't so much that she felt ill, but utterly drained of energy and she had the conviction that something terrible was about to happen to her.

Anne told herself not to be stupid and reached out for the glass on the bed-side table, but all the strength seemed to have gone out of her muscles and when she did manage to take a sip, the water wouldn't go down and she half choked, tears streaming down her cheeks as the liquid came down her nose. She lay back on the pillows, struggling to get her breath, and looked across at the alarm-clock. Its face was blurred and she blinked her eyes, trying desperately to focus, but she was seeing everything double and as she closed her eyes again, she had the appalling insight that unless she got help within a few short minutes, she was going to die.

Anne opened her mouth to shout, but there was no power in her voice and all that came out was a hoarse groan. She tried to get out of bed, but with every passing minute, she was getting weaker. She rolled sideways, falling to the floor half caught up in the bedclothes, and tried to free herself so that she could crawl towards the door. She managed to get half-way there, ignoring the pain from her finger, the nail of which had been half ripped off, before her strength finally gave out and she lay face down, gasping for breath.

'Oh God!' she whispered. 'Somebody help me, please!'

* * *

Sue Kemp came briskly up the corridor, swinging her handbag and smiling to herself. The bag was a nice touch, she thought, but nevertheless it had been stupid of her to have told the lie about the cinema; suppose Anne were to ask her about the film? What would her friend say if she knew that not only had she been only a few yards away in her room, but what she had been up to and with whom? The answer, she had to admit, was that Anne would almost certainly forgive her, which in many ways made it so much worse. She excused herself by thinking that if her friend persisted in her Victorian attitude towards men, then she had only herself to blame if she couldn't keep her boy-friends, but deep down, she was ashamed of her behaviour. At that moment, though, she wasn't considering that too seriously; it had needed a lot of thought and planning to persuade Simon in the first place, but he was certainly making up for lost time now.

She knocked on Anne's door and when there was no reply, seeing that the light was still on, gently eased it open.

She had only moved it a few inches before it hit an obstruction; she pushed harder and finally got it open wide enough to look inside.

'Oh no!'

2

Roger Newton was lying on his back enjoying the feel of the hot sun on his face, when a pair of small hands gripped his hair and pulled hard. He let out a shout of surprise, disentangled himself with some difficulty and then lifted the small boy high above his head and shook him gently.

'You little devil! You'll be the death of your aging father one of these days.'

He lay back again and began to rock backwards and forwards, the baby letting out parrot-like shrieks of delight, and caught the eye of the girl reclining on the deck chair. He gave her a wide smile and when she responded, felt a warm glow deep inside himself, wondering, not for the first time, how he could ever have considered himself to be a confirmed bachelor. He raised one eyebrow and inclined his head in the direction of the house.

Alison Newton smiled. 'Two minds with but a single thought. I'll see if I can persuade junior to have his sleep.'

* * *

'Oh Hell!' said Newton, stretching an arm across to the telephone on the bed-side table. 'The blasted thing hasn't rung all weekend; why does it have to do so now, of all times?'

'Let it ring.'

'Might as well deal with it. Yes,' he said irritably into the instrument.

'Newton?' barked the familiar voice of his chief at the Yard. 'Osborne here.'

Newton made a face at the girl lying beside him, who grinned back at him wickedly before burrowing beneath the bedclothes.

'Good afternoon, sir.'

'I always mistrust you when you're in one of your polite moods,' he rasped. 'What's that?'

'Nothing, sir.'

Alison Newton raised her head momentarily, then buried it again as she saw the anguished expression on her husband's face.

'You sound most peculiar — must be the line. Look, that fellow Golding has just been on the phone, thinks he's come up with something at St Christopher's Hospital. You're our resident hospital expert and I want you to go to see him first thing tomorrow morning — he'll tell you all about it then.'

Newton swallowed painfully. 'Oh my God!' he whispered hoarsely.

'Are you sure you're all right?'

'Just trying to stop a sneeze.' Newton just managed to get the receiver back before he burst out laughing. 'You'll get me suspended from the Force for disrespect to my seniors, you will. You know what happens to naughty girls who interfere with police officers in the course of their duty, don't you?'

'Is that a threat or a promise?'

'What do you think?'

When she saw his expression, she tried desperately to get away, but he caught hold of her ankle, pinned her down and raised his hand in the air.

Alison twisted her head round and looked up at him. 'No! Please Roger, no!'

He gave her a faint grin and the prodigious slap rang out like a pistol shot.

⋆ ⋆ ⋆

Golding, the forensic pathologist, was fiddling with a film projector when Newton went into his office.

'Ah, there you are. Don't shut the door. Miss Graves!' he bellowed.

The defeated-looking woman, whom Newton had seen crouched anxiously over her typewriter in the front office, put her head cautiously round the door.

'Two coffees, Miss Graves.' Golding looked at her departing back with an expression of distaste. 'Always looks as if she's just crawled out of one,' he said loudly. 'Can't think why I put up with her.' He intercepted the detective's disapproving look. 'I suppose you're wondering why she puts up with me.'

'The thought had crossed my mind.'

'Well, I'll tell you — it's because she

doesn't believe that I mean half the things I say about her.'

'Do you?'

'I'm not a man given to saying things lightly — can't afford to in my profession.'

Newton wondered, not for the first time, if Golding was really such an arrogant and conceited ass as he seemed and after due consideration, again not for the first time, came to the conclusion that he was. There was no denying, though, that he was the best forensic pathologist in the country.

'It can hardly have escaped your notice, Inspector,' he said, when they had settled down with their coffee, 'that the worst 'flu epidemic of the decade is sweeping the country.'

'It's true that I'm neither totally blind nor deaf, Dr Golding.'

However hard he tried to resist it, Newton often found himself answering the pathologist in kind and he always regretted it afterwards, but the man never seemed to notice it, probably because he wasn't listening, being too busy concentrating on the sound of his own voice.

'Well, there have been a number of cases of sudden death associated with it and I decided to look into the problem. I have examined all the ones in London with the greatest care and have arrived at a satisfactory conclusion in all of them, until the last one of all — a young nurse who died at St Christopher's Hospital on Thursday of last week.'

'Why do people die suddenly in 'flu epidemics?'

Golding put the tips of his fingers together. 'In some, it has nothing to do with the 'flu itself — some ten people die suddenly of heart attacks in London alone every day — in others, the stress of the infection may precipitate such an attack.'

'But what about young people?'

'I was coming to that. A super-added bacterial infection, such as staphylococcal pneumonia, may be so fulminating that the patient dies in a matter of hours; encephalitis, an inflammation of the brain due to the virus, may do the same thing, and finally, there may be an acute carditis — the heart muscle just fails to function adequately under the influence of the infecting agent.'

'What about this nurse, then?'

'Ah yes, now her case is very interesting. Initially, despite the most searching of tests, I was unable to find a cause of death. The clinical notes were non-existent, but there was a needle puncture mark and a small bruise on her left upper arm and enquiry revealed that she had had an injection of 'flu vaccine some two or three hours before she died.'

'But can't vaccines occasionally cause death? I'm sure I've read about it in connection with smallpox and a number of other conditions for that matter.'

'You're quite right, but not only would the timing have been wrong in this case, but when I injected a mouse with a sample of the girl's blood, some very peculiar things happened to it. Look!'

The pathologist pulled down the blinds and Newton moved his chair round so that he could see the white screen, which had been set up against the wall.

'Those two mice are from the same litter — one has been injected with the girl's blood and the other with some of mine. At first, as you see, they are both running about quite normally — now, look what happened an hour and a half or so later.'

It was obvious that one of the mice was having difficulty with its balance; when it tried to turn, it fell on its side and took a long time to right itself. Within a few more minutes, it was dragging its hind legs, which kept splaying apart and before long it fell on its side, its breathing became progressively more laboured, until finally it gave one last twitch and lay still.

Golding switched off the machine and released the blinds. 'I won't bore you with the details, but I tried various dilution experiments and the inescapable conclusion is that that girl died as the result of a massive dose of a most powerful toxin.'

'Any idea which one?'

'Well, as it looked as if it had been introduced at the time of her 'flu injection, I had to think of one that would have been powerful enough to have paralysed and killed mice in low concentrations twenty-four hours after the girl died. It was my view that there was only one poison that would fulfill all these criteria and some further experiments proved it to my satisfaction.'

'I see, and what was the verdict?'

'Botulinus toxin. I immunised a mouse with the anti-toxin and it survived a dose which was lethal to an unprotected animal. There is no doubt in my mind that that girl died as the result of it — I can even tell you the strain, it was the A.'

'I've heard of the stuff, but that's about all. Isn't it the most potent poison known?'

'You are a positive mine of information, my dear Newton. It is indeed; less than one millionth part of a gram is enough to kill a man.'

'But couldn't she have got it from a natural source? I'd always believed it to be a type of food poisoning. Isn't botulinus the Latin for a sausage?'

'Is there no limit to the man's knowledge? What it is to have the benefits of a classical education — it is a pleasure to talk to you.' Newton looked up to the heavens and sighed audibly, but the pathologist didn't seem to have noticed anything. 'Yes, you're quite right; the toxin is produced by a bacillus, but certain conditions are necessary for its production and the greatest danger is in contaminated tinned foods which have not been sterilized properly. The bacillus itself is not dangerous and fresh food is never the culprit. I'm not saying that she couldn't have picked it up naturally, but if she did, she must have had a tin of contaminated food in her room, which she did not share with anyone else.'

'How common is this sort of poisoning?'

'In this country, almost unheard of; commercial canning involves the use of sterilizing methods which effectively eliminate the risk. In the majority of cases, home-made cooked foods are the source of the trouble. I suppose you might find some half eaten paté in her room sent by a well-meaning aunt, but for my money, that injection was the most likely way for the poison to have been introduced — the timing's about right too.'

'What is the cause of death in these cases?'

'In the main, the toxin acts on the voluntary motor nerve endings and interferes with the release of the normal chemicals that cause muscle contraction.'

'Producing paralysis?'

'Precisely. The muscles around the face and those of the respiratory apparatus are particularly affected; death would be most unpleasant as consciousness is not lost until respiration ceases.'

'Is there no treatment?'

'Antitoxin, in the way I showed in those mice, will neutralize any of the poison still circulating, but once it is bound to the cells, one can only try to keep the patient going until the toxin is dispersed naturally and even then, there may be severe difficulties as the nervous control of the heart and gut may be affected.'

'What a horrible way to die!'

'I can certainly think of more pleasant ones.'

'If you are correct in your view, is there any chance that the 'flu vaccine might have become contaminated by accident?'

'No, is the short answer to that.'

'And how available is this stuff?'

'It is used in some laboratories specializing in toxicology and also occasionally in physiological experiments, but I don't know if anyone at St Christopher's is engaged on work like that at the moment.'

Newton nodded his head pensively and got out of his chair. 'Thanks very much — there doesn't seem to be much doubt about it.'

'There is none.'

The two men shook hands and when the detective had reached the door, Golding was already sitting behind his desk and beginning to light his pipe.

'Oh Newton,' he said when the Inspector was almost out of the room, a faint smile twisting his lips, 'I thought you might be interested to know that that girl had had a pregnancy, probably within the last year — someone terminated it for her, too.'

* * *

'Well, George, we're off to another hospital.'

Newton saw Sergeant Wainwright's ill-concealed grin and shook his head with mock severity. 'We'll have to do a darned sight better than we did last time.'

'I wouldn't have said that you did too badly in the end, sir.'

Newton had a vivid mental picture of how close he and Alison had been to dying in the concrete bunker on the golf course and shivered slightly.

'That's true enough, but it was no thanks to our combined efforts.'

'What's the problem this time?'

Newton told him in a few crisp sentences.

'I see. What's the plan? Same as last time?'

'Yes, I think so. I've already made an appointment for us to see the Hospital Secretary later this morning; we can then have a general look round and play the next step by ear.' He glanced at his watch. 'We better be on our way.'

As the man preceded him out of the room, Newton looked at Wainwright's massive shoulders, wondering how his suit stood up to the strain; the material was stretched to bursting point and the seam at the back had pulled apart slightly. He liked working with Wainwright; the man may not have been one of the brightest members of the CID, but he was good-hearted, reliable and his presence seemed to have an inhibitory effect on people, particularly the more violent members of the community. More than once, he had been sure that men they had been about to arrest were ready to give in to the temptation to mix it, but one look at the sergeant balanced lightly on the balls of his feet had caused an abrupt change of mind. Newton also liked to think aloud when on a case and Wainwright had the knack of making exactly the right noises, saying neither too little nor too much. The last reason why he could on occasions be so valuable was only too obvious when Newton intercepted a look that one of the typists gave the man as they walked down the corridor.

* * *

Robin Styles had only been secretary of St Christopher's Hospital for a couple of years; since the reorganization of the Health Service, the post was of less importance than formerly, but even so, there were times when the responsibility hung heavily on his shoulders. This was just such an occasion. Denis Poynter, the senior physician and chairman of the medical advisory committee, was at his most tiresome, doing everything he could to needle the Chief Nursing Officer, Miss Beale. His views about her were quite simple; St Christopher's had had a Matron for over a hundred years and what's more, a Matron who wore a uniform and was respected, and he had no time for the droopy-shouldered spinster in her dreary cotton dress, who, to his way of thinking, would have been more at home selling raffle tickets at a church bazaar.

'If you ask me,' he said loudly, 'it's all a lot of fuss about nothing. I can't think why the police have been brought into a perfectly straightforward case like this — every time vaccinations are carried out on a large scale, one gets the odd death. It's always a tragedy of course, but one has to remember that the procedure may save hundreds of lives.' He looked up suddenly. 'Unless, of course, Matron, there was something fishy about Nurse Wilkinson.'

Every time she met him, Miss Beale did her best to prevent her hackles from rising, but once again she failed. The emphasis he put on the word 'matron', a title which she disliked and in any case no longer existed at St Christopher's, always succeeded in irritating her profoundly.

'And what is that supposed to mean, Dr Poynter?'

The physician shrugged his shoulders and smiled maliciously. 'If her death was due to natural causes, why in that case would the flat-footed brigade be tramping through these hallowed portals?'

'I know Anne Wilkinson's mother personally — we were staff nurses at St Gregory's together — and you have no right . . .'

The pitch of her voice had risen several tones and Styles decided that the time had come to do something about the situation before the two of them sprang at each other's throats.

'Don't you think it would be better if we waited until we hear what Inspector Newton has to say?' He looked at his wrist watch. 'He should be here any minute now.'

Miss Beale was sitting bolt upright and he could see her knuckles white as she pressed her fingers tightly together. There was an uneasy silence and Styles gave a start when the internal telephone suddenly began to ring loudly.

'Styles, here . . . Splendid, show him in, will you please?'

Poynter was used to bullying people; in fact he got a good deal of pleasure out of it. He bullied his wife, his junior staff, the students and his patients, all with equal enthusiasm and even those of his colleagues who did not depend on his influence, soon found that crossing swords with him was an unrewarding pastime. Whenever they were rash enough to do so, they almost invariably lost their tempers and became upset, while Poynter clearly thrived on a diet of rows and arguments.

He got up as soon as the two men entered the room and decided to make his position clear right from the start.

'I don't know what all this is about, Inspector, but with this 'flu epidemic everyone here is very busy.'

If he was expecting an apology, or even a conciliatory reply from the tall, dark-haired man in his late thirties, he was sadly disappointed. The detective looked at him with his level grey eyes for what seemed a very long time and then with a ghost of a smile said:

'I don't think we've been introduced. My name is Newton and this is my assistant Sergeant Wainwright.'

Styles tried to wipe the grin off his face as he saw Poynter's expression and rapidly introduced himself and the two others. Newton waited until the Hospital Secretary had poured out the coffee and then looked round at the three people facing him.

'Of course I realize just how busy everyone here must be, but the reason we're here is that the coroner is not satisfied about the cause of Anne

Wilkinson's death.'

Poynter had another try. 'Come, come Inspector, let's not have any beating about the bush; in what way exactly?'

'She was poisoned by botulinus toxin and we have to find out how it came about.'

Newton had not originally intended to tell them straight away, but had quickly decided that the only way to get any co-operation out of the peppery physician was to use shock tactics. His remark certainly had an effect; Poynter's mouth dropped open and some of the colour left his cheeks.

'That's ridiculous — there hasn't been a case in this country for years.'

'I know.' Newton paused for a moment and looked round once more. 'We think it was given to her deliberately.'

'You mean she was murdered.'

'That's right.'

'Who says so?'

'Dr Golding, the forensic pathologist.'

'But that's quite absurd. Who would want to poison a junior nurse with something like that?'

'That is precisely what I intend to find out.'

'You can be certain that you will receive every possible assistance, Inspector,' said Miss Beale, throwing a triumphant glance in Poynter's direction, 'at least from the nursing staff.'

All the bounce seemed suddenly to have gone out of the senior physician; he almost appeared to have shrunk physically as he rose from his chair.

'I'll leave the arrangements to you, Styles — if there are any difficulties, let me know.'

'I'd rather that this information wasn't passed around just yet, Dr Poynter,' said Newton. 'It'll only frighten people and make our job more difficult — I'm as anxious not to cause unnecessary disruption as you are.'

'Very well.'

He gave the Inspector's proffered hand the merest touch, nodded to the others and walked out. There was an awkward silence after he had left; Miss Beale appeared about to say something, but then seemed to think better of it and

Styles shuffled nervously through the papers on his desk.

'How were you proposing to set about your enquiry, Inspector?'

'As a start, I would like to have a word with the girl who found Nurse Wilkinson, if I may, and then we'll see how we go. Is there an interview room I could have?'

'Of course. I'll do something about that and Miss Beale, perhaps you would be kind enough to arrange for the girl to be sent down?'

3

'I won't keep you long, Miss Kemp; I expect Miss Beale told you that we are making some enquiries into Anne Wilkinson's tragic death.'

'You can take as long as you like, Inspector, it'll get me out of having to give Mr Hayes a blanket bath — he weighs a ton and he's always complaining.'

After only a couple of minutes, Newton was quite sure that Wainwright would get more of the sort of information he wanted out of the girl in ten minutes than he would in a couple of hours. Sue Kemp wasn't pretty in the conventional sense of the word — her mouth was too wide and her complexion was rather muddy — but within a few moments of entering the room, Newton was sure that she had summed them both up and he had little doubt about the conclusions she had come to. She kept running her forefinger through her dark hair, constantly replacing an errant lock behind her right ear and every time she did so, shot a glance in Wainwright's direction.

'You were the one who found her, weren't you?' The girl nodded. 'Did you know her well?'

'I suppose you could say she was my best friend — at least amongst the nurses.'

She paused just a fraction too long and the suggestive smile she gave confirmed Newton's opinion of her.

'Would you tell me what happened?'

'There's not much to tell really. I saw Anne after supper and as she looked rotten, suggested that she went to bed early. I offered to sit with her or send for the Home Sister, but she wouldn't hear of it and when I found that her temperature was normal, I decided to keep my date. Three hours or so later, I looked in again to see how she was and found her on the floor. She must have crawled out of bed because she was right up against the door — I had quite a job getting in.'

'Was she still alive when you found

her?' The girl gave a shudder and shook her head. 'I believe that you all had a 'flu vaccine that afternoon; was anyone upset by it?'

'One or two of us had sore arms, but I haven't heard of anyone being really bad. Was it that that killed her then?'

'It's one of the possibilities we're looking into. Were you there when she had her injection?'

'No, I had mine with an earlier group.'

'Who did the injecting?'

'Dr Forrester, one of the medical registrars — at least, he did mine.'

Newton looked at his watch. 'Would you excuse me, Miss Kemp, I have to make a phone call? Sergeant Wainwright would like to ask you a few more questions. George, may I have a word with you outside for a moment?'

'What's up, sir?'

'I want you to find out a lot more about that murdered girl — you know, personal details — and I have an instinct that you're the man to dig them out of that femme fatale in there.'

'You don't like her, do you sir?'

'George, you're getting positively psychic in your old age. No, I do not; I cannot match your Olympian detachment in these matters, however hard I try.' The sergeant grinned and put his hand on the door handle. 'And George, don't forget to ask about her eating habits.'

'Eating habits, sir?'

'Yes, tainted duck paste in the wardrobe.' Wainwright looked at him as if he had gone insane. 'I'm sorry, George, I forgot to tell you; you can pick up this toxin by eating contaminated food — find out if she was in the habit of going in for midnight feasts in the dorm.'

'The dorm, sir?'

'George, this echolalia is beginning to get me down. Dorm, d-o-r-m, short for dormitory, but then I was forgetting, you never had the dubious advantages of a boarding school education. I just want to know if she liked to supplement her diet in the privacy of her room. Have you got it, or shall I put it another way?'

'No, that's all right, sir,' said Wainwright cheerfully, 'the message has been received.'

'Good. Meet me in 'The Blue Boar' at twelve forty-five, it's in that quiet square across the road from the main entrance to the hospital.'

* * *

'Phew! He's a bit forbidding, isn't he?'

'Oh, he's all right once you get to know him.'

George Wainwright forced himself to take his eyes off the girl's legs, of which she was showing a good deal more than when Newton had been in the room, and sat down behind the desk.

'It must have been a great shock finding your best friend like that.'

'It was. You know, Anne and I used to have long arguments about religion — she was ever so keen and was always trying to convert me — and it hardly seems fair that something so horrible should have happened to a girl like her. Now, if it had been someone like me . . . '

'How do you mean?'

'Well, I like a good time, you know.'

Sue Kemp licked her lips and looked across at him.

'I was referring to Anne Wilkinson,' said Wainwright, swallowing painfully. 'As if you didn't know,' he added to himself.

'Of course — silly me. It was just that she was so good; it made me feel guilty sometimes just to look at her. People didn't swear when she was about, she never had a bad word to say about anyone and she was always prepared to do an extra turn to help out.

'Did the other girls like her?'

'Not really, she made them feel uncomfortable.'

'Did she have any boy friends?'

Even though the pause was slight, Wainwright was quite certain that she hesitated fractionally before replying.

'Well, she used to go out sometimes with one of the medical students — he's also a Christian Union type — but nothing ever happened, if you know what I mean.'

'Go on. In this day and age — you must be joking.'

'No, really. I knew Anne backwards and

she was going to wait until she got married — don't make any mistake about that.'

'What was the name of this bloke?'

'Why do you ask?'

This time, Wainwright was absolutely certain that the girl was uneasy.

'Just trying to build up a picture of the poor girl — we always do this when someone dies unexpectedly.' He could see that she was unconvinced and decided to try another tack. 'Have a lot of people here got the 'flu?'

Sue Kemp stopped fiddling with the hem of her dress and looked up, he could have sworn with relief.

'I think the worst is over now; the vaccine arrived a bit late to do any good.'

'I suppose it has meant a lot of extra work for those left.'

'I'll say.'

'Do they look after you well here? What's the food like?'

'It's all right, but a bit expensive; at least on our salaries, we think so.'

'The pathologist thinks that Anne might have died of food poisoning; did she go in for private stores in her room?'

'Good Lord no, it's against the rules.'

Wainright laughed. 'I can't see that deterring hungry nurses.'

'You didn't know Anne.'

⋆ ⋆ ⋆

When Wainwright put his head into the saloon bar, Newton was already occupying a seat in a quiet corner of the room.

'Get yourself a drink and something to eat, George, and then you can tell me how you got on.'

The sergeant elbowed his way through the crowd standing around the bar and returned a few minutes later with a pint and a large pork pie. He sat down, took a long draught from his glass and wiped his mouth with the back of his hand.

'That's better.'

'How was it then? Uncover any dark secrets?'

Wainwright gave him a detailed account of the interview.

'Well now, George, that's very interesting.'

The sergeant took another long drink.

‘Oh, I thought it was very disappointing. This girl Anne Wilkinson seems to have been whiter than white — hardly the type to get herself murdered.’

‘Ah, but you see, George, I know something about her that you don’t. According to Golding — and he doesn’t make mistakes about this sort of thing — the girl had had a fairly recent pregnancy, probably terminated, and unless you believe in parthenogenesis, it is a question of ‘cherchez l’homme’.’

Wainwright thought and hoped he knew what Newton was talking about, but wasn’t sure and put on what he fondly imagined was an expression of interest. Newton wasn’t fooled for an instant and seeing his look of blank incomprehension, decided not to make matters worse by trying to explain.

‘What about the medical student boy friend that Susan Kemp mentioned?’

‘I deliberately didn’t press her about him; you see, I was quite sure that she regretted having let that piece of information slip out. When I first started to talk to her, she was fruiting around a bit

— you know what I mean, showing a lot of leg, giving me the old eye and making vaguely suggestive remarks — but when the question of this bloke came up, she quite suddenly shut it all off. I tried to get more out of her later on, but there was nothing doing. Oh yes, there was one last thing, I did ask her about whether Anne Wilkinson kept any food in her room and it seems pretty clear that she didn't — evidently she was a girl who always stuck to the rules.'

'I never did think anything of that food poisoning idea.'

'How did you get on, sir?'

'Badly. Both the registrar and the Home Sister are off with the 'flu and the nursing authorities were unable to tell me anything about Anne Wilkinson other than the fact that she was a good and reliable nurse and a few details about her family background, which was conventional enough in all conscience. Her father's a general practitioner in Worthing and her mother was a staff nurse at St Gregory's before she was married.'

'What are you going to do now?'

'Before you gave me your news, I was somewhat devoid of ideas, but now I think a few discreet enquiries at the medical school would do no harm. I'd like you to chat up the Head Porter — he'll probably be a useful ally — then go through Anne Wilkinson's room with a fine-tooth comb; luckily with the staff shortages, her things haven't been packed up yet. See if you can find any clues to her personal life — you know, letters and that sort of thing. I've already cleared it with Miss Beale. I'd also like you to find out where that girl had her abortion; I believe that some sort of register is kept these days, although I suppose it's possible that she had it done illegally.'

* * *

Newton took an immediate liking to Renfrew, the Medical School Secretary. It didn't require a Professor Higgins, the detective thought, to identify him as an ex-RAMC colonel. He was an alert, sandy-haired man of about sixty, with a neat moustache and wearing a comfortable tweed suit, which seemed to have remarkable fire-proof properties. Whenever he got up to do something or answered the phone, he stuffed his evil-smelling pipe into one of the capacious pockets, even though it was still alight, and Newton watched fascinated as a thin plume of smoke issued from inside each time he did it.

'Well, Inspector, what can I do for you?'

'One of the nurses here, a girl called Anne Wilkinson, died suddenly a few days ago. The forensic pathologist has determined the cause as being due to poisoning with botulinus toxin and thinks that it was probably injected at the time she was given the 'flu vaccine. I might say that only Mr Styles, Miss Beale and Dr Poynter know of our suspicions and I am most anxious that the information doesn't travel around the whole hospital.'

'I see, and where do I come in?'

'I have been unable to see the registrar, Dr Forrester, yet — he's the person who did the injection and is away with the 'flu himself — but one of the other nurses, a friend of Anne Wilkinson, told us that she had a medical student boy friend. For some reason, she was not at all keen to give us his name and rather than press her at this stage, I wondered if you could help.'

Renfrew chewed reflectively on his pipe. 'This complicates the issue more than somewhat.' He picked up the telephone. 'Miss Barnes . . . I don't want to be disturbed for the next half hour. If there are any callers on the phone perhaps you'd tell them that I'll ring back later.' He replaced the receiver and leaned back in his seat. 'You'll understand, Inspector, that life can be difficult for students and those in medical schools are no different from any others; in some ways they have even greater problems, particularly those at the pre-clinical stage. They have a long period of study ahead of them with no prospect of any real independence or of making any money for a good five years, they have only just left school, have often never been away from home before and are trying to grow up emotionally, all at the same time. You will not be surprised to hear that all this is too much for some of them. I suppose you could say that I'm something of a father confessor to them and get to know pretty quickly which ones are going to have special difficulties. I had my eye on Simon Buxton right from the moment I first interviewed him; you see . . .'

⋆ ⋆ ⋆

Simon Buxton's mother was married in her middle thirties to a man almost double her age. Her husband did all that was expected of him; he gave her a child, died, as he did everything else, quietly and with the minimum of fuss before he became old enough to become a problem to look after, and he left her comfortably off.

Alice Buxton looked upon her son as a kind of superior doll, to be put on show, dressed up and fussed over. For the first five years of his life, almost his only social contacts were with the middle-aged women who came to his mother's bridge parties and who were in the habit of ruffling his hair and dutifully saying what a pretty little boy he was.

For Simon, school was a type of refined misery; the other boys bullied him and even though he was good at his work, the teaching staff thought him insufferably wet. At times, he was so utterly dejected that if it hadn't been for the local vicar, Michael Rushton, he might even have committed suicide. Here, at last, was someone he could treat as a father, someone who was prepared to talk to him as an equal, someone in whom he could confide and with whom he could discuss his fears, hopes and ambitions.

There could be no denying that Rushton liked small boys, but that was as far as it went. Even though he was a man of iron self-control, he had not managed to exorcise that particular devil with complete success until he got married. He was well aware that if he, as a bachelor, tried to organize scout troups and boys' clubs, he would be the target for the gossips and scandalmongers, so he set out to find exactly the right wife. Mary fitted the bill to perfection; she worshipped him, never questioned what he asked of her physically and even managed to look like a boy.

It was hardly surprising that Simon Buxton should have modelled himself on the man he so much admired. As time went by, he gradually developed more self confidence; he enjoyed helping Rushton with the scout troup — what a revelation it was to have the younger boys looking up to him for a change — and the vicar's particular brand of dogmatic Christianity suited him down to the ground.

When Simon went up to medical school in London, Rushton found him lodgings with a friend of his, who had more than enough room in his vicarage, and he settled down happily enough. It was only natural that he should have gravitated towards the Christian Union and it was there that he met Anne Wilkinson. Up to that time, Simon had had absolutely no contact with girls and was scared stiff of them, largely because of his almost total ignorance of sexual matters. It was one of the subjects he had never discussed with Rushton and the talks at school, which had been done extremely badly, embarrassed him profoundly.

His relief when he discovered that Anne was quite happy to accept him as a friend with no sexual overtones at all, was enormous — at least it was for a time. In the few months following his arrival, he saw a lot of her at the Christian Union meetings and discussion groups and at last, greatly daring, he asked her out to a coffee bar. It was on that occasion that he discovered feelings for her that refused to go away, however hard he tried to hide them. If she had responded at all favourably to his first tentative physical approach, all might have been different, but when he tried to hold her hand the first time he took her out to the cinema, she jumped as if she had been bitten by a snake. Perhaps, not surprisingly, some of the others had their eyes on the couple.

'Those two make me sick,' Peter Spencer, one of the senior students, said in the common room one evening.

'Who?'

'Héloise and Abelard over there.' He pointed across the room. 'Do you see what they're drinking? A tomato juice and a bitter lemon — I ask you, I don't know what this place is coming to. Come to think of it, those nicknames aren't in the least suitable — I can't see the worthy Simon being any good in the seduction stakes.'

Sue Kemp laughed. 'Oh, I don't know; I reckon he's got hidden fires.'

'Fancy him yourself, do you? I bet you anything you like that you wouldn't be able to make it with him.'

'I might just take you up on that one day.'

The more Sue Kemp thought about it, the more excited she became at the idea — it would be a challenge worthy of her talents. Anne was all right in her own way, but she was a sanctimonious prig and if Simon got to know what a bit of real action was like, it might do them both a bit of good.

Her opportunity came at the leaving party which was being given for one of the staff nurses who was leaving nursing to take up full-time modelling. There were about thirty of them there on the stage at the end of the students' common room and it started, as these parties usually did, quietly enough, with groups of people chatting together, but as the alcohol began to flow, so did the noise level rise. Sue Kemp had managed to slip some vodka into Simon's tomato juice on a couple of occasions and made sure that she didn't leave his side. She was racking her brains, trying to think up a way of getting rid of Anne Wilkinson, who was standing quietly nearby, when a cheer went up from the other side of the room.

'Come on, Carole, give us a preview,' someone shouted.

The girl was lifted up on top of a table and everyone settled down on the floor to watch her impromptu strip-tease. All of them, that was, except for Anne, who started to make for one of the fire exits at the back of the stage.

'Are you coming, Simon?'

Sue held him tightly by the hand and for a fatal moment he hesitated. He was feeling light-headed and his heart was hammering with excitement at the prospect of what was going to happen, and he allowed himself to be pulled down on to the carpet beside her. Even though Carole got no further than her bra and pants, he found this more arousing than if she had stripped off altogether and there was no ignoring the warm proximity of the girl next to him, nor the things that she was making his hands do to her. He didn't really remember exactly how he got into the small ante-room with Sue, but by the time he had sobered up sufficiently to realize what was about to happen, it was too late. He made a half-hearted attempt to get away, but the almost naked girl lying on the cushions on the floor sat up and her whisper came through to him quite clearly.

'Simon, if you walk out now, I'll scream.'

She held out her hand towards him and he was lost.

The following morning, Simon Buxton was consumed with guilt, but the hospital padre happened to be away on that day and his intention to talk it over with a confessor was frustrated both by that and the fact that Sue Kemp took him to her room again that afternoon.

As the devoted adherents of Pavlov in the KGB had found to their advantage and before them, at a less profane level, the followers of Wesley, there are few greater enthusiasts than those who have been converted from one way of life to another almost diametrically opposed to it. Simon Buxton saw Sue Kemp whenever he could, which was on most days; he took to propping up the bar in the students' club and totally neglected his former friends and interests. If Anne Wilkinson knew what he was up to, or was upset by his behaviour, she never showed it. She made no attempt to seek him out and on the rare occasions that they met in the corridor, she smiled pleasantly and did not try to avoid him.

When Simon heard about Anne's death, particularly when he found out exactly when it had occurred and what he had been doing at the time, the effects on him were quite shattering. The full enormity of his behaviour suddenly struck him and he was able to come to only one conclusion; he was utterly wicked and did not deserve to live. He went back to his lodgings, took the bottle of sleeping pills out of the medicine cabinet in the bathroom and swallowed the lot.

* * *

Alan Renfrew knocked his pipe out in the heavy glass ash tray. 'The poor fellow was far too distraught to have planned it with any care; he was found within an hour or two and no real harm was done. He told me the whole sad story when he came round.'

'Well, clearly a visit from me will do nothing to hasten his convalescence; I imagine that his mental balance must be on something of a knife edge.'

'I can't tell you how relieved I am to hear you say that, Inspector. Of course I can do absolutely nothing to stop you seeing him if it's really essential, but I gather from our psychiatrists that it will be touch and go. A lot of young men and women of that age are rather delicate plants, particularly those going in for higher education; they have been so busy studying that they have neglected to grow up and of course religion and sex are two of their biggest problems — you don't have to look further than Simon Buxton to see that.'

'Poor fellow. He certainly doesn't appear to have had any reason for wanting to kill Anne Wilkinson — Sue Kemp I could have understood — and if you would be good enough to find out where he was at the time of the fatal injection, I think we'll be able to leave him in peace, providing, of course, he was somewhere else at the time.'

'When was it exactly?'

'Between five and five-thirty last Thursday.'

Renfrew made a note on the pad in front of him. 'That shouldn't be too difficult — I'll let you know.'

'I suppose you didn't happen to know this girl Anne Wilkinson at all?'

'No, but I do just remember her father — he was a student when I was a houseman here. One of my jobs is to keep up the register of old students; I'll look him up for you. It won't take a moment.' He flicked through the bulky loose-leaf book which was on the table at the side of the room. 'Yes, here we are. Let's see; ah yes, I remember now, he's a GP in Hove and a leading light in the anti-abortion campaign.'

'Is he now?'

Renfrew looked up sharply. 'You're not going to tell me that she was pregnant, are you?'

'No, but she had been and the forensic chap seems to be pretty sure that it was terminated artificially and fairly recently at that.'

The secretary whistled. 'I'd be willing to bet anything that Simon wasn't responsible. The man was in a state of shock when he spoke to me; I've seen that sort of thing often enough in the army during the war and I would swear that not only was he telling me the truth, but quite literally the whole truth.'

'I don't doubt it. Probably her experience was the explanation for her attitude towards men, but it hardly seems a very adequate reason for anyone wanting to murder her.' Newton got up. 'Well, I've used up enough of your time; thanks for your help.'

'Not at all. If you want to ask anything else, feel free to drop in whenever you like.'

'Thanks, I will. Oh, by the way, there was just one more thing. Do you have much contact with the medical staff?'

'Yes, I frequently have lunch in the consultants' dining room and I sit on several of the joint hospital and medical school committees. Why do you ask?'

'Well, botulinus toxin is hardly something that you could pick up at the local chemist and I was wondering if you might be able to find out for me if anyone is using it for research purposes in the hospital, without making the enquiry too obvious, that is. It's probably a pious hope and I clearly won't be able to keep it quiet for long, but at the moment I don't want our murderer to know that we have caught on to his method.'

'I'll have a try.'

Renfrew opened the door to the office and glanced at the note which his secretary had left in front of her typewriter.

'Oh God!' he said, 'that's the last straw.'

'What's wrong?'

The secretary smiled. 'Just some medical school trivia; it's the staff-student golf match tomorrow and our best player has cried off — another victim of the 'flu. I don't think I'm going to be able to raise a side.'

Newton resisted the temptation for about five seconds. 'I don't know whether I would qualify as a member of the honorary staff, but I play a bit.'

'My dear fellow, do you? You're positively manna from Heaven; you can play with me — no one else will. Wranbury Common at 9.30 tomorrow then?' Newton nodded. 'I have an instinct about you — single figure?'

'Five.'

Renfrew grunted contentedly. 'We'll show 'em this time; I'm only sixteen, but I play to it.'

4

Roger Newton crept up behind the girl standing in front of the cooker and kissed her on the nape of the neck. She gave a sudden start and dropped the wooden spoon she was holding.

'Roger, you'll be the death of me. Look, it's gone all down the front of my clean blouse.'

He dipped his finger into the saucepan and put it into his mouth.

'Urgh . . . What on earth's that?'

'Delicious soup for your supper. I made it myself and it's got all the fresh vegetables you're so fond of in it, swede, turnip, parsnip . . . '

'Stop!' He put his hands to his stomach and tottered round the kitchen, groaning horribly. 'Poison!' he gasped and collapsed in a heap on a chair.

'Relax, it's only for Michael. He loves it.'

'He can't do.'

'I assure you, he does and so do I for that matter — not everyone's as faddy as you are. I put all the bits and pieces into the liquidizer and hey presto!' She laughed at his expression of disgust and opened the oven. 'Despair not — how about this?'

The cheese soufflé was excellent and with the baby asleep, they settled down in the sitting room with their coffee.

'How did it go?'

He told her in detail what had happened during the day. 'As is so often the way, nothing seems to fit at all at the moment, but then we've hardly started. I think that chap Renfrew's going to prove very useful — not only is he someone in whom I have complete trust, but he's both discreet and very perceptive I think.'

'I suppose that's your excuse for playing golf tomorrow.'

He frowned at her with mock severity. 'One of them, but another is that Poynter is also playing. He reacted in a most peculiar way when I saw him with the Hospital Secretary and Miss Beale, and I want to know why. It's absolutely infuriating so many people being off with the 'flu — I was unable to interview either Forrester, the medical registrar, or the Home Sister and Sue Kemp didn't see Anne receive her injection. Any comments? You know the nursing setup so much better than I do.'

Alison Newton thought for a long time. 'Not really, except that I can't see a nurse using a poison like that; I for one have never even heard of it and it must be very difficult to come by. There is one thing, though.'

'What's that?'

'I can remember having a vaccine — also for the 'flu in fact — and all the syringes were filled in advance; we filed past a trolley and the doctor giving us the injections lifted them up one by one as the need arose. If the poison was administered by that method, then I don't see how anyone other than the registrar or the nurse filling the syringes could have made certain that the right girl got it.'

'I see your point; I must confess that I hadn't realized how it was done. It makes it all the more important for me to see that registrar so that I can find out exactly what happened at that trolley. The trouble is that he's gone home to convalesce — his parents live somewhere in Gloucestershire — and it rather looks as if I'll have to go down there the day after tomorrow. He's not expected back at work until next week.'

'What about the Home Sister?'

'She's also away from the hospital with 'flu and is evidently pretty ill, so I didn't feel I could insist on seeing her today.'

'How about George? Did he dig up anything fresh — apart from Sue Kemp that is?'

Newton laughed. 'Poor George, it's not really fair to set him loose amongst all those man-hungry nurses, it upsets him — natural inclinations against duty and all that. No, in fact he found nothing out of the ordinary in her room at all. Anne Wilkinson was a regular Bible reader and had quite a few other religious books about, but no caches of tinned food and no dark secrets such as supplies of the contraceptive pill. He's going to try to find out where she had the abortion tomorrow.'

⋆ ⋆ ⋆

It didn't take Newton many minutes to realize that he and Renfrew were going to make a formidable combination in the foursomes. The Medical School Secretary seldom hit the ball more than a hundred and sixty yards — he didn't use wooden clubs at all — but every shot went dead straight and he was rock steady on and around the greens. He seldom put any approach putt further than two feet from the cup and was utterly resolute when it was his turn to hole the short ones. In a little over two and a half hours, Newton and his partner were round in seventy-seven and had defeated their bemused opponents by six and five, winning the bye three and one for good measure.

'My God, I enjoyed that,' said Renfrew as they took their pints out of the clubhouse and stood by the eighteenth green watching the other players. 'It makes such a change to play one's second shots at some of the longer par fours with at least a chance of reaching the green.'

'Well, you're certainly deadly from a hundred and fifty yards down; it was your tee shot at the short twelfth that really demoralized them.

'Ah yes, but what wouldn't I give to be able to hit a drive two hundred and fifty yards occasionally. Every time I hit the ball with a wood, it sails miles out to the right; I know what I'm doing wrong, at least I think I do, but it's too late to do anything about it now.'

Newton shaded his eyes against the sun. 'Isn't that Dr Poynter approaching?'

'I can't quite make out, but I'll know as soon as he plays his shot — I'd recognize his swing a mile off, it could fairly be described as individual.'

The last hole at Wranbury Common was a shortish par four, three hundred and eighty-nine yards long. The green was guarded by three deep bunkers, which meant that the second shot had either to be played high on to the green with plenty of stop on it, or more riskily, pitched on to the apron, just beyond the bunkers, and allowed to run on.

Both drives of the approaching four-somes were good ones and Newton could see the two balls lying side by side on the fairway some one hundred and forty yards short of the flag.

'Come along, Newton, this is going to be worth watching. Poynter's got to play the second shot and knowing him, he'll make a hash of it and if the match is close, that will hardly endear him to his partner.'

'Who's he playing with?'

'Raymond — one of the pathologists. Apart from you, he's our best player and luckily a very good tempered bloke; he'll need to be if this match is really tight — mark my words.'

The two men walked up the fairway and when they reached the group of players, Renfrew had a word with one of the students. He came back rubbing his hands and smiling broadly.

'Just as I'd hoped; they're all square.'

The students' ball was some five yards behind the other and the young man took a seven iron out of his bag.

'Delusions of grandeur,' whispered Renfrew, 'he'll never make it.'

He was right. Although perfectly struck, the shot was never long enough; the ball rose high in the air, landed with a loud thump ten yards short of the cross bunkers and must have hit a hard patch of ground, for it bounced all of twenty feet into the air, cleared the sand and stopped on the edge of the green.

Poynter clicked his tongue. 'Bloody lucky!' he said under his breath, but loud enough for everyone to hear. Then, with a flourish, he took out his three iron.

'Don't you think it would be wiser to play short; we don't want to go into those bunkers, they're absolute hell.'

'Look here, Raymond, are you playing this shot, or am I?'

After a lot of grumbling the senior physician was finally persuaded to take out his number seven.

'Just play it quietly and I should be able to pitch it up close enough to give us a good chance of a four.'

Poynter's swing was like nothing that Newton had ever seen before. Someone in the past must have told him to pause at the top of his back-swing and he had obviously taken this instruction very much to heart. Once the club-head was pointing to the sky, he froze as if doing a more than passable impression of Lot's wife, and after an interminable wait, brought it down with a frenzied heave. The club, with its face closed, hit the top half of the ball, which took off, never rising more than a couple of feet and making a noise like an enraged wasp, as its torn cover clove the air. It bounced twice on the hard ground and then buried itself into the face of the middle of the three bunkers in front of the green.

'What did I tell you, Raymond? If I'd used the three iron, all would have been well.'

The pathologist let out a long-suffering sigh, smiled wanly at Renfrew and before shouldering his bag, took out his sand-iron. Just short of the bunkers, he lit up a cheroot and contemplated the half-hidden ball for a full minute.

'That's a sure sign of what he's thinking,' whispered Renfrew. 'He always gets one of those stinking things going when he's nervous.'

Considering everything, the shot he played out of the bunker was little short of miraculous. The long-suffering ball, which had a gaping cut in it, was half-buried under the lip of the trap and Raymond had to stand with his left foot a good eighteen inches above his right. A fraction of a second after completing his stroke, he fell back into the sand, but the ball came out well, bounced on to the green and rolled to within two feet of the hole.

His effort drew warm applause from the small group of people watching and as he brushed the sand out of his hair, the pathologist gave Renfrew a wink. The student's approach from just off the edge of the green was an extremely weak one and not only did they have to putt first, but were left with an extremely tricky eight footer.

'I do hope he slots this one,' Renfrew said, 'I'd give a lot to see Poynter have to hole that short one to save the match.'

His wish was granted. The student was

clearly a man of decision and iron nerve; he walked straight up to the ball and without studying the line or asking for the other ball to be removed, struck it in as casually as if he had been playing against his grandmother on the back lawn.

When Poynter walked towards his ball, everyone thought that he was going to putt, but instead, he picked it up, put it into his pocket and turned towards his opponents with a smile and with his hand outstretched.

'Match halved then — good contest.'

There was an awkward silence and then the senior of the two students, although colouring slightly, stood his ground.

'But we didn't concede that putt, sir. It's our match.'

Poynter's mouth dropped open and a purple flush began to spread up his neck, but before he could get a word out, Raymond stepped forward with a brand new ball and placed it roughly where the other one had been.

'Quite right, partner,' he said loudly, 'you can't be expected to putt with that wreck of a ball you had there — you're allowed to change it on the green.'

The student seemed to speak again, but Raymond said something sharply under his breath and gradually the tension subsided.

'Christ!' said Renfrew. 'That was a close call. I hope to God he gets it in; if he misses the whole day'll be ruined.'

It must have taken Poynter all of three minutes to settle down to that putt. He inspected the ball as if it had been booby-trapped, he studied the line from every angle and even when he did take up his stance, he seemed incapable of bringing the club back. Finally, when it seemed that he was never going to take the plunge, he gave the ball a convulsive stab. If he had hit it with the full face of the club, the ball would have gone straight back into the bunker, but he only managed to graze the very top of it and with agonizing slowness, it trickled towards the hole and with its very last turn, dropped in.

'Well holed, old chap — that deserves a whisky if ever anything did.' Raymond put his arm round the physician's shoulders and started towards the club-house. 'And what about you two?' he said, looking across at their opponents, who were standing looking pale and shaken at the side of the green. 'Pints?'

Renfrew slowly let out his breath as the tension visibly relaxed. Raymond was still talking loudly, praising the students for their brave putting, and as he disappeared into the bar, the secretary stabbed the air with his pipe.

'That man Raymond's a bloody marvel. There's not another person on the staff who could have salvaged that situation — I still feel quite weak at the knees.'

'I don't get it,' said Newton.

'Get what?'

'Poynter. I've only met him twice and on both occasions he's been rude and aggressive to people who aren't really in a position to answer back — the man's obviously a cheat and a bully; how come he's managed to get away with it for all these years?'

'Oh, he's not such a bad sort really and you've seen him at his worst; he doesn't always behave like this and my guess is that the business of this nurse has upset him tremendously.' Renfrew laughed when he saw Newton's expression. 'No, I'm not suggesting that he had anything to do with it.'

Newton was dying to ask him exactly what he did mean, but the secretary had begun to fiddle with his pipe and by the time he had got it going, they were in the club-house.

The relaxed atmosphere both in the bar and at lunch was entirely due to Raymond. He seemed to be everywhere, cracking a joke one minute and buying drinks the next; the man's good humour was infectious and the incident on the eighteenth green was soon forgotten.

'In fact Raymond's your man if you want to find out about botulinus toxin,' Renfrew said in an undertone as lunch was drawing to a close, 'he's the Professor of Microbiology. I would be quite prepared to ask him myself, but for the life of me I can't think up a convincing reason for doing so.'

'Is there any chance of me playing with

him this afternoon?'

'Like to size him up yourself, no doubt. Well, it can be arranged easily enough, but the snag is that I'll have to play with Poynter.' Renfrew raised his eyes heavenwards.

'By the looks of him you'll have to carry him round.'

'Don't you believe it. What he's had to drink will just serve to steady him up nicely.'

It was quite true. Although Newton had seen the man put away four double whiskies, he behaved quite differently after lunch. He nodded affably at the detective, asked him how his enquiries were going and even his swing seemed to have speeded up as he launched a perfectly respectable drive from the first tee.

Newton enjoyed the afternoon round even more than the one in the morning. He soon discovered that Raymond had played for Cambridge a few years before he had been in the Oxford team and they had many mutual golfing acquaintances. As he chatted to the pathologist between shots, he realized how foreign to the man's true nature his extraordinary performance at lunch must have been. In fact, he was a quiet soft-spoken man with a dry sense of humour and a fund of golfing stories.

Although they both played well, they had to give their opponents twelve strokes and in the event, it was just too much for them and they lost on the seventeenth green. After the match, Newton managed to manoeuvre his partner into a quiet corner of the bar and brought over a pot of tea and some scones.

'You know that Alan Renfrew told you that I was a friend of his and was just making up the number?' The pathologist nodded. 'Well, it isn't strictly true; I'm from the CID and I'm looking into the death of one of the nurses; she died suddenly the evening after having had a 'flu vaccine and the pathologist who did the autopsy is convinced that she was murdered by an injection of botulinus toxin.' Raymond took a box of cheroots out of his pocket and offered the detective one. 'No thanks.'

'Who was the pathologist?' he said when he had got his cigar going.

'Golding.'

'I might have guessed. If he's right, it's a very smart piece of work indeed — I must ask him how he did it.'

'You know him then?'

'Yes, the field is a fairly small one and we keep in touch at the various meetings.'

'This toxin must be pretty difficult to get hold of; is there any in the hospital?'

'Yes, as a matter of fact there is; one of the neurobiologists in my department is working on it at the moment.'

'How accessible is it?'

'As far as I know it's just kept in one of the lab fridges.'

'Isn't that rather asking for trouble?'

'No, I don't think so. I haven't actually seen it myself, but no doubt it's kept in one of those bottles with a diaphragm on top; that means that the liquid can only be removed through a needle and if the whole thing's properly labelled, I would have thought that there was adequate safeguard. You must remember that that particular fridge is only ever used by trained research workers.'

Considering that botulin was the most toxic substance known, Newton thought that this was a somewhat casual approach, to say the least of it, but decided that there was nothing to be gained by pointing that out.

'Where is this fridge located?'

'In the corridor that connects the various labs. The neurobiology department shares a floor with the chemical pathologists and as we're very short of space, we have to make use of every available square inch.'

'Is it kept locked?'

'At night, yes, but not during the day.'

'How easy would it be for someone to get at the bottle?'

'There'd be no difficulty at all provided that whoever it was knew where to look, and at certain times of the day, in the lunch hour for example, there's no one much about.'

'In the normal course of events, how many people would handle the bottle?'

'I'm afraid I don't know, it's nothing to do with my particular line of research;

you'd better ask Anderson, he's the senior lecturer actually doing the work.'

'Thanks, I'll get my assistant to look into it tomorrow.'

'Are you making any headway?'

'Just getting the feel of things at the moment. I hope to find out a bit more when I see Forrester, the medical registrar, tomorrow. He's convalescing from the 'flu at his parents' home.'

'I hope it all goes well for you.' The pathologist got out of his chair. 'Well, I'm afraid I must be getting home; I must say I've enjoyed today enormously, not least this afternoon. I very much hope that we'll be able to play again one day. Give me a ring at the hospital if the opportunity arises.'

'Thanks, I will.'

They shook hands and as the detective turned towards the locker room, he was pulled up short by the penetrating voice that came from across the room.

'Newton! Come here a moment, will you?' He turned and saw Poynter sitting in a corner by himself, a large whisky on the table in front of him. 'What'll it be?'

A drink was the last thing that Newton wanted, but this, the first even vaguely friendly approach from the physician, was too good to miss.

'Thanks, I'll have a lager.'

'Mark it up to me at the bar, will you, there's a good chap? I don't think I could walk another inch; thirty-six holes in one day, even foursomes, is, at my advanced age, more than I can really manage.'

When Newton got back, he saw that Poynter was in worse shape than he had realized; his speech was slightly slurred and he seemed to be having difficulty in focussing clearly.

'I want to apologize to you, young man.'

'Apologize? Whatever for?'

'I must have appeared very unwelcoming when you came to the hospital yesterday — the fact is that this business has hit me hard, very hard indeed.' He took a sip of his whisky and peered at the detective as if he was looking at him through frosted glass. 'Looking at me you'd think I'd been to a public school, wouldn't you? Winchester perhaps? New

College, Oxford?' Newton nodded. 'Well, you'd be wrong. My father was a clerk in local government and I went to a grammar school in South East London. You've had a chance to see what St Christopher's is like by now; it may still seem like one of the last bastions of privilege, but I assure you it was ten times worse when I was a student before the war. Can you imagine what it was like for a young boy without money and an accent you could cut with a knife; not that anyone did anything so ill-bred as to laugh at me to my face, but there are many worse ways of being ridiculed than that. Everything was so much more formal in those days, you know, dinner jackets even for the monthly dances we used to hold and all that sort of thing.

'It was the war, of course, that was the making of me in more ways than one. I went into the RAMC and got left behind in France after Dunkirk. I managed to bring back a boat-load of chaps from Brittany and most of them were wounded. To be honest, it was sheer luck; I chanced to run into the owner of a fishing boat who happened to be an ardent Gaullist and while he did most of the hard work, I got the kudos. Stories like that were ten a penny at that time, but mine happened to be taken up by the press and that's how old Arthur Ponsonby got to hear about it.'

The physician paused and went off into a private reverie.

'Who was he?'

Poynter came to with a start. 'Old Ponsonby? He was one of the senior physicians at St Christopher's and officer in command of a medical division at that time. I had my membership, he wanted me to work with him and that was that. I went to Germany for the latter part of the war, finished up a colonel and after a short period as RMO at St Christopher's after it was all over, was put on to the staff. By then, of course, the social climate was changing, a lot of the crustier and more formal physicians and surgeons had left and there was I, the ex-grammar-school-boy, a member of the Establishment.

'Ambition's a funny thing, you know; lots of people have found that all the pleasure is in getting there and very little when one is standing on the top of the heap, and certainly it was true as far as I was concerned; I had to find other worlds to conquer. I became Dean of the medical school, for a long time was a member of the General Medical Council, and only a few months ago, I heard that a knighthood was in the offing. A lot of people sneer at honours, but I know for a fact that they're hardly ever turned down and it would have been one thing that I could have taken into my retirement. And now it's all over.'

He sighed deeply and reached for his glass.

'Why do you say that?'

'Because this case is going to make the headlines and any hint of scandal in the hospital, particularly if it involves one of the senior staff, will tip the balance. I know, I've seen it happen before.'

'What makes you think it's a senior member of the staff?'

Poynter wasn't listening; he just peered into the middle distance, shaking his head slowly.

'Finished. When the baby died and my wife was unable to have any more, all my hopes of having a son — one who didn't have to start with the disadvantages I had to face — went with the wind. I suppose it was inevitable that my good fortune wouldn't last. I married late, but we were so happy before Edith got depressed.' He choked and blew his nose loudly. 'Sorry — had too much to drink.'

'How are you going to get home?'

'What do you mean?'

Newton wasn't prepared to get involved in an argument over the physician's competence to drive and went across to the bar where Renfrew was sitting with a couple of the students.

'I'm afraid Poynter's had a skinful — we can't possibly let him drive home.'

'You're quite right, of course,' Renfrew replied when he had looked across towards the physician. 'He looks as if he's asleep already. I tell you what, I'll drive him home in his car and tuck him up in bed. One of the students can take mine back; I'd better not let them have Poynter's Rolls — it would frighten the living daylights out of them. To tell you the truth, I can think of more relaxing occupations than conducting £12,000 worth of machinery into the heart of Chelsea. Would you believe it, Poynter's got one of those personalized number plates as well — now that's a form of vanity I never could understand. Do you know, our obstetrician — a silly fellow if ever there was one — had OBS 1 on his car. The students changed it to UPU 2 and he didn't notice it for a week. Served the silly bugger right.'

It was quite a task getting all Poynter's kit, and for that matter the physician himself, into the Rolls without making it too obvious that the man was quite incapable of even walking on his own, but eventually they managed it and when the student had been organized, Newton watched the two cars out of sight with a thoughtful frown on his face.

5

'Yes, this is Dr Forrester.'

'My name is Newton, Inspector Newton of the CID. I'm sorry to disturb you when I know you've been ill, but one of your patients has been found dead and we think she's been murdered.'

'What was the name?'

'I'd rather not discuss it over the phone; I was wondering if I might come to see you tomorrow some time.'

'Why not come to lunch? Hang on a second, I'd better check with my mother first.' The man was only gone for a couple of minutes. 'Yes, that would be fine — about 12.30 suit you?'

'Yes, thanks.'

'Do you know this part of the world?'

'Not all that well.'

'It's quite simple; you come in on the A 40 and then . . . '

* * *

Forrester's parents lived in a modest semi-detached house on the outskirts of Cheltenham, but there was nothing modest about the welcome given by his mother, a large comfortable Scotswoman. She was obviously dedicated to the proposition that her son needed feeding up and Newton could see the force of the argument. The man was tall and thin and looked grey and ill. He only picked at the excellent steak and kidney pie and refused the sweet altogether. Newton's healthy appetite obviously made him a great favourite in Mrs Forrester's eyes and she beamed delightedly as he polished off a second helping of the apricot flan.

'Well, you two will be wanting to get down to business; I'll leave you in peace.'

She brought them coffee in the living-room and smiled warmly at the detective as she bustled out.

'Your mother certainly knows how to cook; I haven't had such a good lunch for years.'

Forrester smiled. 'I'm afraid that I'm a sad disappointment to her; I have a poor appetite at the best of times and I must say this ’flu has knocked me sideways.’

‘Yes, it does seem to be pretty virulent; I’ve been lucky so far.’

‘You said on the phone that one of my patients had been murdered.’

‘Yes, I’m afraid so — one of the nurses, a girl called Anne Wilkinson.’

Newton thought the man was going to faint. What little colour there had been in his face had disappeared and he could see the drops of sweat standing out on his forehead.

‘Yes, she was found dead last Thursday evening.’

Forrester made a tremendous effort to control himself. ‘That was the day my father came to fetch me from the hospital. I hadn’t been feeling well ever since I woke that morning and I knew that I was sickening for the ’flu. I live alone in London, you see and . . . ’ His voice trailed off.

‘We are almost sure that she was poisoned when she had her anti-’flu vaccine.’

The man half-rose to his feet. ‘You’re not trying to suggest that I had anything . . . ’

‘We think that someone may have

substituted one of the syringes. That's why I wanted to see you, so that I could find out exactly what happened. I don't suppose you remember injecting Anne Wilkinson, do you?'

Forrester licked his lips nervously and thought for a moment.

'As a matter of fact I do. As I told you, I wasn't feeling at all well myself, but everything was going perfectly satisfactorily until Dr Poynter arrived with a whole crowd of consultants and started to make a fuss, generally getting in the way and trying to organize everything differently. Anyway, after he and the others had moved away, I was pretty fed up and was a bit careless with the next injection — nothing much, I just hurt the girl a bit — and she promptly fainted. There was quite a panic and after a couple of the other nurses had carried her on to a couch, I started again. I remember that Anne was next because the Home Sister snapped at her, something she was always doing.'

'Why? Didn't she like her for some reason?'

Forrester looked uncomfortable, then seemed to take a decision. 'Well, the poor girl's dead, so it won't do her any harm if I tell you about it, but it would upset her parents terribly if they found out, so if you can see your way to keeping it quiet . . . ' Newton nodded reassuringly. 'About seven months ago, Anne came to see me in a dreadful state of distress; a few weeks earlier she had been on her way back from the cinema alone when some lout pulled her into the garden of a disused house and raped her. She was bruised and badly shocked, of course, but not seriously hurt and she didn't tell a soul about it at the time. Her reason for coming to see me was that she found herself pregnant.'

'Why ever didn't she tell someone about it before?'

'It's not so surprising; she hadn't seen her attacker properly and you can imagine what all the publicity would have done to her. I hadn't known her before, but it was obvious that she was rather straight-laced herself and with the most puritanical parents.'

‘Why did she come to you?’

‘I don’t really know, perhaps it was because we were working on the same ward.’

‘What did you do?’

‘I had no hesitation in arranging for a termination at St Gregory’s; she was seen by one of their psychiatrists, a chap with whom I was at medical school, and it was all done quickly and without fuss.’

‘How did she react to it herself? I understand that her father is a prominent anti-abortion man.’

‘Well, she was terribly upset by the whole business, but I think she was as happy with the decision as anyone could be.’

‘Where did the Home Sister come in?’

‘She’s a sanctimonious bitch, if you’ll pardon my language. When she heard about it, she told me that she was quite sure that Anne was making up the whole story, just so that she could get an abortion.’

‘Why ever should she want to say a thing like that?’

‘If you want my opinion, I think she

had been just a bit too fond of Anne and had probably been given the brush-off. For all her Christian ideals, that woman's a thoroughly bad lot and a positive menace in the position she holds.'

'How did she find out about it?'

'Don't ask me — I didn't tell her and certainly advised Anne not to either; I felt that the fewer people who knew about it the better. In fact, she had the operation done during a week's holiday and Miss Heywood — she's the Home Sister — came out with it a few weeks later. She even had the brass to imply that I was responsible for the pregnancy.'

'What was your reaction to that?'

'I told her that if she cared to repeat it in front of a witness, I'd sue her and be glad of the publicity. That soon settled her hash.'

'Well, that clears up the matter of Anne Wilkinson's pregnancy, which I knew about as the result of the autopsy, but as to the reason why anyone should want to murder her, that's quite another matter. Do you have any theories yourself?'

'I can't say that I have. I hardly knew

her of course, but she seemed very straight forward — a thoroughly nice girl in fact.'

'Now, how about those injections? Would you tell me in detail how you went about them?'

'Not much to tell really. The syringes and needles, all of which were disposable, were loaded by one of the casualty staff nurses and I threw the used ones into a rubbish bin. I suppose she must have kept about six ready at any one time, depending on how fast the queue was moving.'

'How many people were close to the trolley you were using?'

'Well, Sister Heywood, the staff nurse and I were there the whole time, but I can't recall anyone else except when Dr Poynter and all the others came in, then there must have been at least a dozen people milling around.'

'Can you remember who they were?'

'I'm afraid not; at that particular moment I was feeling under the weather, overworked and quite frankly was having great difficulty in keeping my temper.

Poynter always manages to irritate me profoundly.'

'Do you happen to know the name of the staff nurse?'

Forrester shook his head. 'You shouldn't have any difficulty in finding her, she works regularly in casualty and she's got rather striking red hair.'

Newton talked to him for another half hour, but managed to get very little further information. He left Forrester in the sitting room and said goodbye to his mother at the front door.

'Thank you so much, that was a simply marvellous lunch.'

'It's so nice to see someone enjoying their food for a change,' she said rather wistfully. 'You must come again some time.'

'I'm sorely tempted.'

As he reached the front gate, Newton turned suddenly and saw Forrester's pale face staring at him through the sitting-room window. The man smiled and lifted his hand, then the curtain dropped back into place.

* * *

Newton was in luck when he called in at the psychiatric department of St Gregory's Hospital. Christopher Bailey, the registrar who had dealt with Anne Wilkinson's case, had just finished his clinic and was dictating his letters. The detective couldn't suppress a faint grin when he introduced himself — yet another of his cherished medical illusions had been shattered. Somehow, he always expected psychiatrists to look, if not exactly like Sigmund Freud, at least like one of his nephews, and to speak with thick central European accents. In fact, Bailey was a very trendy young man indeed, who would have looked perfectly at home as the manager of a successful boutique.

'I'm sorry to arrive out of the blue like this,' said Newton when he had explained what he wanted to know, 'but I'm sure you appreciate that we have to move as quickly as possible.'

'I'm afraid that I can't remember her case all that well without her notes. Would you excuse me a moment while I go and fetch them?'

He was gone a good twenty minutes and having interviewed a good few doctors in his time, Newton would have been prepared to make a small bet that he had made a swift phone call to his defence organization. At one time he had been irritated by what had seemed to be obstruction and lack of will to help on the part of some of the medical profession, but with increasing experience and particularly since he had been married to Alison, he had come to recognize that their patients came first in their reckoning and rightly so.

His enquiries must have reassured him, because when he returned, the psychiatrist could not have been more helpful.

'I remember her very well now that I see the notes. She told me exactly the same story that you got from Duncan Forrester and as she was a nurse and as one still has to be rather careful over these matters, I got her seen by one of our consultants. He agreed with me that a termination was justified and it was done within a few days.'

‘It seemed a straight forward enough case then?’

‘Yes, it would have been if she had been telling us the whole truth.’

‘How do you mean?’

‘It’s not entirely a question of being wise after the event; I made a note at the time, I see. One gets to know when people are lying — I have no doubt that you find the same in your job. It’s often difficult to say how one knows, but in this case the girl’s story was just a little too pat, a little too well rehearsed, if you know what I mean. At any rate, I didn’t think it would help if I probed too deeply and if her way of coping with a traumatic situation like that was to make up a story then that was all right by me. I knew, of course, about her parents and felt that an illegitimate baby would lead to a serious risk of suicide.’

‘Did you ever discover the truth?’

‘Not entirely, but when I saw her a few weeks after the operation to make sure that she had got over the experience satisfactorily, she broke down and gave me most of the details. She really was on the way back from the cinema alone and she was pushed into a garden, but she clearly believed that what happened next was at least partly her fault. You see, she recognized the man and seemed to think that she could have stopped him quite easily if she had really wanted to. What appalled her was that not only did she not want to stop him, but the pleasure she had got out of the whole incident. I know that that sounds a bit far-fetched and the idea that a girl can enjoy rape has been grossly over-sold in the past, but the fact is that she did and, what's more, couldn't stop thinking about it. Coming to terms with one's own sexuality can be a pretty traumatic business, particularly for a girl with her upbringing, but after a few sessions, she seemed to have done so very satisfactorily.'

'Did she ever tell you who the man was?'

'No, but she made it clear that she had had nothing further to do with him and that he didn't suspect that she knew who he was.'

'What an extraordinary story.'

The psychiatrist smiled. 'You wouldn't say that if you sat in at my clinics for a week or two.'

'Do you think that what she finally told you was the truth?'

'Yes, I do.'

'What about the man? Didn't you think that it was dangerous to let a rapist get clean away with it?'

'No, Anne convinced me that not only would he be most unlikely to do it again, but if she exposed him, it would have been a very long time after the event and it would also have meant stirring up the sort of publicity she knew she could never face.'

Newton tried to press him further, having a shrewd suspicion that the psychiatrist knew the identity of Anne Wilkinson's attacker, but he refused to be drawn.

* * *

Before returning home, Newton called in at his office at the Yard and found George Wainwright waiting for him.

'How did you get on, sir?'

'So, so. How about you?'

'I found Dr Anderson all right and he showed me round their laboratory. The place is an absolute bloody shambles, you've never seen such a mess. You can hardly walk along the corridor without knocking into bottles, filing cabinets, lockers and I don't know what else besides. Anyway, he told me that he hadn't touched that toxin for a week or two and the bottle was in a separate plastic container, which was clearly labelled with Anderson's name and also had a 'poison' notice on the outside.'

'Lots of prints on it?'

'No, both the bottle and the box had been wiped absolutely clean; it must have been done earlier that morning because the fridge is in constant use and Anderson told me he was quite certain that he had moved the container the previous evening — he wanted a bottle behind it.'

'Who uses that particular fridge?'

'Just Anderson and his two technicians.'

'How widely was it known that he was working on botulinus toxin?'

'I did ask that and he told me that he'd given a talk on it to the hospital research club only a month earlier.'

'Good work, George. Incidentally, that abortion was done at St Gregory's.' He saw the sergeant's face drop. 'I'm sorry, I only found out at lunch time.'

Wainwright wasn't going to let on to the fact that he had got the same information at the cost of a mere couple of phone calls and made the most of it, sighing deeply.

'To think of the hours I spent tramping the streets yesterday.'

'Come off it, George, don't overdo it; you'll have me in tears before you've finished. You have to appear in court tomorrow morning, don't you?'

'No, I heard earlier this afternoon that it had been put off.'

'Good, in that case you can come with me to St Christopher's tomorrow and give me a hand. I'm planning to lay on a little reconstruction of the crime and I'll also tackle the Home Sister provided she's well enough.'

'O.K.'

'Fine. I've got to put Osborne in the picture now. See you.'

* * *

Newton sat back in his favourite armchair with a contented sigh, cupped the mug of hot chocolate with both hands and put his feet up on the pouffe.

'Well come on; don't keep me on tenterhooks any longer. How did it go?'

When he was first married, Roger Newton had deliberately avoided bringing up the subject of his work when at home, but soon found that not only was Alison genuinely interested in what he was doing, but quite often contributed ideas of her own. He marshalled his thoughts for a moment and then told her about his visit to Forrester and the psychiatrist at St Gregory's and what George Wainwright had told him.

'Even before I saw that psychiatrist, I thought there was something funny about Forrester's story; I noticed it when he was talking to me in fact. It wasn't so much what he said, but his tone of voice. I wasn't happy about that rape business either — it didn't seem to me that a girl like Anne Wilkinson would have behaved in that way.'

'Oh I don't know; if I'd been in her position and hadn't been badly hurt, I might have done just the same. Just think of all the miserable consequences of going to the police; even if the courts had kept her name out of it, everyone in the hospital would have known, you can bet your bottom dollar on that.'

'Yes, that's true. The psychiatrist's story was interesting, though.'

'I suppose you're wondering if Forrester did the raping and then fixed up the abortion in a fit of remorse.'

'It's certainly a possibility.'

'But even if that were correct, it hardly seems an adequate reason for killing her and so long afterwards.'

'No, I agree, unless she was a blackmailer, which I must say doesn't ring true at all. For that matter, she seems an extremely unlikely target for a premeditated murder. Everyone, that is Forrester, Miss Beale, Sue Kemp and Renfrew gave me the impression that she was a nice, conventional girl, a bit pi for some people's tastes, but without any malice in her.'

'Did Forrester seem absolutely shattered when you told him that she had been murdered?'

'Yes, he did and I could swear that he wasn't acting. I don't think there can be any doubt either that he did catch the 'flu — he looked absolutely terrible.'

'What about the medical student?'

'Simon Buxton? I think we can rule him right out — I discovered that he was helping another student with a physiology experiment at the time of the injection.'

'Can you think of any other possible motive?'

'I can't say that I can, unless we're dealing with a complete maniac, in which case there may not be one at all. I'll just have to see what that Home Sister has to say in the morning; George found out that she was transferred to the nurses' sick bay at the hospital this morning.' He yawned and stretched his arms. 'How about a spot of bed?'

* * *

The following morning at breakfast Alison Newton seemed unusually quiet and preoccupied and after his second request for the marmalade had been ignored, the detective looked anxiously across the table at her.

'What's up, love? You feeling all right?'

She gave him a smile. 'I'm sorry, Roger, I haven't been able to get that case of yours out of my mind ever since I woke up and I've just thought of something. Suppose Anne Wilkinson's murder was a mistake?'

'What?'

'You said that Forrester was so annoyed by the arrival of Poynter and his retinue that he injected one of the girls rather roughly and she promptly fainted.' He nodded. 'Well, if the next girl in the queue went to her aid, which is very likely, mightn't the poisoned injection have been given to the wrong person?'

Newton let it sink in for a moment, then got up and gave his wife a hug. 'Would you believe it, that idea never even occurred to me and the more I think about it, the better I like it. I certainly had thought that the whole business sounded very hit and miss, but I suppose the killer might easily have been able to think up some excuse for being near to the trolley at that particular moment, even without the good fortune of a whole crowd of people arriving at the psychological moment. We must also remember that if it hadn't been for Golding's exceptional ability, a murder would never have been suspected, so that the risk of it being discovered would have been minimal. Of course you realize the implication of what you've just said?'

'Yes, and I only hope that you're not too late.'

'So do I.'

6

Caroline Ford woke up early, feeling clear-headed for the first time for several days. When she got up, she had a momentary spasm of vertigo, sitting down again abruptly on the edge of the bed, but all her aches and pains had gone and she knew, without taking it, that her temperature had returned to normal.

Even her appetite had come back and after a bath, she put on a clean nightie and boiled herself an egg, made some toast and sat down in the kitchen. The 'flu could hardly have come at a worse time, just when her plans were beginning to work out; still, she would be able to get back to the hospital within a day or two and then . . . She allowed herself the luxury of a long day-dream, thinking how much life had changed for her in just two short years.

* * *

Ever since she could remember, Caroline Ford had hated everything about her home and the town in which she had lived all her life. When her father was out of prison, which was a mercifully infrequent occurrence, life was even more unpleasant for them all than when he was inside, when, although they were chronically short of money, at least they were protected from his violence. When he was sober, he was morose and used to beat them at the slightest provocation and when he was drunk, he tried to hit them even harder, but then his aim was bad and half the time the furniture suffered as much damage as they did.

As far as the house was concerned, it had almost no redeeming features; being scheduled for destruction, no one was prepared to do anything about the place which was slowly falling to pieces about their ears. The paper was peeling off the walls, the double bed which she shared with her two sisters, was damp and throughout the whole house there was the smell of decay.

Unlike her brothers and sisters, who

played truant more often than not, and spent their days wandering around the streets, making quite a business out of shop lifting, Caroline found school the one thing that made life tolerable. It was warm, it was dry and she got one square meal a day. At home, her mother had long since given up any attempt at cooking proper meals and was slowly eating herself into a premature grave; she spent the whole day drifting around the house in her broken down carpet slippers, munching biscuits and sweets, getting progressively fatter and more short of breath as the weary months went by.

For almost as long as she could remember, Caroline had had a burning desire to get away from the whole family, all of whom she despised, the stinking house and the wretched town with its permanently grey and sulphurous atmosphere. If it hadn't been for Miss Lacey, she would never have achieved it. The majority of the children at the school were in some way deprived, discipline was a nightmare and the responsiveness of the occasional pupil was one of the things that kept the middle-aged spinster going. Caroline was one of those; she was bright, if she had been properly fed and washed she would have been pretty, and she had a quiet determination to do well. Miss Lacey, who had left her job in London to return home to look after her old and invalid mother, first noticed the girl when she had come into her form at the age of thirteen and soon started to let her come back to her house to do her homework. Before long, she was regularly giving the girl high tea and even made sure that she had a bath once a week. Inevitably, she soon knew all about the family and Caroline's ambition to leave home and the town as soon as possible, an aim with which she was entirely in sympathy.

When Caroline managed to get several 'O' levels, Miss Lacey had the idea of a nursing career for her protégée. The more she thought about it, the more suitable did it seem; the girl would get the chance to find her feet in London in a supervised hostel, she would earn reasonable money and most important of all, it was something she was very keen to do. Miss

Lacey selected St Christopher's because she had shared a flat some years earlier with one of the sister tutors there, a woman she trusted to keep an eye on the raw, unsophisticated girl.

The schoolmistress worked with Caroline on the interview with more dedication than she had applied to anything else in her life before. She spent hours on the girl's method of speaking, went over all the questions that she might be asked time and time again and when she finally saw her off at the station, felt a warm glow of pride. With freshly washed hair, only a hint of make-up and the new dress they had selected together, she looked as if she had just stepped out of an advert in the *Nursing Times*.

When she started at St Christopher's, Caroline Ford began to enjoy herself for the first time in her life. She had enough to eat, had a room of her own, with a weekly change of sheets, and she found the job fascinating and satisfying. It was true that at times she was lonely — she was still on the defensive about her regional accent and lack of money compared with most of the others — but she slowly began to make friends and never once regretted her decision to leave home.

Caroline had been at the hospital for rather more than two years when she met Ingrid. At that time, the medical ward was full of elderly women with strokes, heart troubles and chronic chest conditions and the appearance of a young patient made a welcome change. When she arrived, Ingrid was confused, irrational and semi-conscious for a lot of the time, but within a few days she began to recover from her attack of virus meningitis and the two girls spent a lot of time chatting together. Caroline had never met anyone before who was either so elegant or so self-assured as the blonde Swedish girl, who seemed to have visited every country in Europe on her modelling assignments.

'Caroline,' she said one day when she was being given a blanket bath by the young nurse, 'would you do me a favour? I left my flat without any clothes and I wondered if you would be kind enough to get them for me and one or two other things as well; I've made a list and written down where everything is. You'll also find a complimentary ticket for Pierre Laennec's fashion show next week; why not go? You'd enjoy it.'

Caroline did wonder why the girl had not had a single visitor and no friends to have brought her things in, but she was glad to help her out and went along to the flat the next day. She had never in her life seen such a collection of clothes as she found in Ingrid's apartment. The flat was quite small, but seemed to her to be the height of luxury and she spent an hour there, trying on dresses, coats and boots and pirouetting in front of the full-length mirror. The whole affair was made all the more exciting by the fact that the clothes fitted her so well and she sampled the expensive perfumes she found on the dressing table and happily day-dreamed the afternoon away. Before she left, she tidied the whole place up, made up the bed with clean sheets and had one last look round.

'One of these days,' she said to herself, 'I'm going to live in a place like this.'

Ingrid stayed in the ward for another week and in that time, Caroline found herself telling the Swedish girl all about the unhappiness of her early life; she had succeeded in hiding her miserable upbringing from the other nurses and it was a relief to be able to pour it all out. When Ingrid was discharged from the hospital, Caroline never expected to hear from her again — she had after all been given the ticket to the fashion show by way of a thank you present — but two weeks later, she received an invitation to spend a weekend in Stockholm. Caroline had never been abroad nor in an aeroplane before and the excitement was almost too much for her.

'Could you use some of these things?' Ingrid said to her in her flat a couple of weeks before they were due to go. 'I'd be getting rid of them in any case.'

Could she use them? Trying to think of the right things to wear on the trip had been a worry to her ever since she had received the invitation and she would never have been able to afford anything even half as nice as the beautiful things she was being offered. Caroline knew that models were highly paid, but she had no idea that they did that well. The fares alone cost more than she earned in a month and she had assumed that they would be staying with Ingrid's parents, but to her amazement, the Swedish girl also had an apartment there, which was just as well appointed as the one in London.

On the Saturday night, they went to a club. Caroline had read about these places and didn't really want to go. It wasn't that she was prudish exactly and even envied Ingrid's totally unselfconscious ability to wander around the flat without a shred of clothing on, but she was still confused about sex, having shut away her few crude, hurried and on one occasion terrifying experiences in company with the rest of her earlier life.

She couldn't have put into words exactly what she expected the club to be like, but it was certainly not the tastefully decorated and obviously expensive place that it was. The first surprise had been to find that they were given VIP treatment by the manager and the second that she found the show neither crude nor sordid and at times very funny. The girls and the two men in it were young and extremely good looking and the large audience, not least the Japanese business man in the front row, whose glasses were removed and hidden in rather an unconventional place, enjoyed it hugely.

'It'll be the day when they allow things like that in London,' she said when they had returned to the flat.

Ingrid smiled. 'They do — maybe not in open clubs, but you can find anything if you know where to look.'

'Go on, you're having me on.'

'No, I'm not. You must have wondered how I managed to live so well.'

'You don't actually . . . '

'Look, Caroline, how much do you earn? A hundred a month after tax?'

'Not that.'

'I get at least three times that in a bad week. Why do you think the manager looked after us so well this evening? I used to work there, you know. I only left because I wanted to learn English and see another country. Why not think about it?'

'I couldn't. For one thing I wouldn't have the nerve and for another, I haven't got a good enough figure.'

'Nonsense, you're just a bit shy, that's all.'

'And what about all the shady characters that one would meet? I've heard stories.'

'All you need is someone who knows the score like I do and you'd have no trouble at all. We're about the same size and we could work together; with me being so fair and you dark, we'd be on to a certain winner. I already have a first-class agent, a woman whom I trust absolutely, and in the last three years in London, I've never even had a moment's anxiety. I tell you what, I'll lay on something really simple for both of us together; at the end of it you'll be fifty pounds richer and if you don't like it, that'll be the end of it. Here, let me show you what you'd have to do; you can be the audience to start with.'

If Caroline hadn't had a few drinks on board, she would never have agreed, but Ingrid put on such a funny act that she did not need too much persuading to try something herself.

The first time on live, all Caroline had to do was pose for some 'photographers'.

'Relax and don't worry,' the Swedish girl whispered as they waited to go on, 'the cameras aren't even loaded.'

The studio was clean, the drapes and the lighting artistic and they were only there for a couple of hours. After she had got over her initial embarrassment, Caroline found that she had a streak of exhibitionism in her that she had suspected in the past, but not admitted to herself, and even began to enjoy it. Having Ingrid there as well made all the difference and afterwards, when they were laughing over some of the men who had been there, she had made up her mind.

She did, though, hesitate before committing herself too deeply and for that reason kept on with nursing, finding it perfectly possible to combine the two activities. She was also able to use her other job as an excuse to avoid getting involved in some of the more way-out things that Ingrid wanted her to do and even though she pulled in nothing like so much money as her friend, she was nevertheless able to put regular sums on one side, which she kept in the small safe in the kitchen of her flat. Moving out of the nurses' hostel had been the first step in her emancipation and within eighteen months she had found a more luxurious apartment and had bought herself a second-hand car.

Everything changed for her again when she was returning from an assignment with Ingrid one evening in a taxi.

'May I borrow your Polaroid camera?' the Swedish girl asked, 'the battery on mine's out.'

'Of course, what do you want it for?'

'Ruth wants me to give her a hand later tonight; she's got a fellow who . . . ' She whispered for a few moments into Caroline's ear.

'He doesn't! How can she?'

'Don't ask me, even I draw the line somewhere. Photography's her special line and she's got some fabulous pictures — she always tries to get an extra one for her collection.'

'I wouldn't have thought that her clients would like that much if they ever found out.'

'That's exactly what I've told her often enough. One of these days something nasty's going to happen to Ruth. You really ought to see them, though, they're out of this world.'

'How does she do it without anyone knowing?'

'Oh, it's easy enough. She has a spare print hidden away that's all fuzzy and she substitutes it for the genuine article after she's done the developing. It's dead simple really, I've seen her do it. There's so much happening after using a Polaroid camera, that anyone could work the trick, particularly as her clients are usually tied up.'

Caroline did see the photographs, a week or two later, and they were all that Ingrid had claimed. There were about fifty altogether and near the end, she came across one that set her heart hammering with excitement. The man was not exactly in a familiar setting — the last time she had seen him he had been walking along the main corridor of the hospital — but his features were unmistakable. She didn't, of course, decide exactly what she was going to do with it there and then, but when she left, the print was nestling safely in her hand bag.

In the preceding eighteen months Caroline had grown to despise the men who paid for their services. They were mostly over forty, obviously well off and she never managed to develop Ingrid's attitude towards them. The Swedish girl clearly enjoyed every minute of her work, claimed to and obviously did like her clients and saw herself as someone giving a useful service, which was well paid, but which she carried out to the very best of her ability.

In fact, when she came to think about it, Caroline realized that she had always hated men. There had been her brothers who bullied her, her father who had at first beaten her and then, when she got older, used to look at her in a way that was even more terrifying, and finally, there had been that occasion, which she preferred to forget, when three of the boys from her school had cornered her on her way back home.

On many occasions she had thought about getting out of it, but the trouble was that she had grown used to having money — she could think of no other way of earning even half as much — and she was genuinely fond of Ingrid and did not want to let her down. Now, as she looked at the photograph, she knew that if she played her cards correctly, the small print would enable her to start a new life; she would finish her nursing training and then, with a really large sum of money behind her, there would be no end to what she could achieve.

The fact that she was calmly considering the blackmail of a member of the hospital staff hardly gave her a qualm. If she thought about it at all, she rationalized it by saying to herself that she was owed a decent life after what she had been through as a child and that the man could perfectly well afford it — she had no intention of being too greedy. Once she had made the decision, Caroline began to study him with meticulous care. She found out where he lived, details of his family life, his salary and the type of car he drove and when she had finished, settled on a sum that was large, but not too large, enough to teach the man a lesson, but not enough to make him desperate.

But would he pay up and how was she going to collect the money without being identified? And supposing the police set a trap? It didn't take much imagination to realize that if once her victim knew who she was, it might just occur to him that the one way of dealing with her would be to silence her for ever, and so she spent many hours trying to work out a fool-proof plan. The one she settled for in the end was rather complicated and would involve her in some risk, but she reckoned that the odds of her getting away with it were acceptable. She would have liked to have gone over the scheme with someone else to make sure that she hadn't failed to see a snag, but that was out of the question.

She was shivering with a mixture of fear and excitement when she finally made her decision and lifted up the phone in her flat.

'Yes,' said a voice abruptly, 'speaking.'

He listened in silence to what she had to say and when she had finished, there was a long pause.

'Ring me back in half an hour; there are people here.'

Having screwed up her courage to make the first call, Caroline very nearly failed to ring up a second time, even though she knew that the mechanism to trace her number could not be set up in the time available. She kept changing her mind, but finally, when the half hour had gone by, she lifted the receiver once more and listened to the ringing tone, her mouth dry with nervous anticipation.

After the first call, the man at the other end of the line sat back in the armchair in his study, ashen faced. He had no doubt that the woman meant what she had said and shaken though he was, he was already planning what to do. He was in fact alone that evening and his decision to ask her to ring back had been instinctive.

When the phone went again, he had his tape recorder set up and kept her on the line for as long as possible. After she had finally rung off, he sat for a long time hunched in his chair. He was quite convinced that she had the photograph — she had given him a full description — and that if it was published, it would destroy him, but if he did pay the sum of money asked, could he trust her to return it and not to have had copies made? He knew that Polaroid prints could be duplicated, but believed that the process was a difficult one and so much depended on whether the girl was working on her own or not. He played through the recording again and was quite sure that it was not the coloured girl who had taken the photograph of him — the accent was quite different. How, though, had he been identified from it?

He was well aware that the police didn't like blackmailers and that if she was caught, his name would be kept out of it, but he didn't really believe that the story wouldn't get out. It would be difficult for him to get hold of as much money as she had asked for, but not impossible, and he was clearly faced with the alternative of paying up and hoping that she would play fair or of making a clean breast of it to the police.

The girl had refused to tell him how she proposed to collect the money, but even a brief consideration of the problem made it obvious that at that time would lie the best chance of catching her. When he started to think hard about whom she might be, a third possibility suddenly occurred to him and however hard he tried to put it out of his mind, it kept returning. If only he could identify her — and he had four weeks in which to do it — he might be able to solve the problem once and for all.

The following day, he rang the hospital to say that he wouldn't be in — with all the 'flu about he knew that no one would question it — but left the house at his normal time. The block of flats in Maida Vale where he had gone to see Ruth, the coloured girl, was broken down and dilapidated and he sensed what must have happened as soon as he saw that her name had disappeared from the row of cardboard strips at the side of the bell pushes. Nevertheless, he walked up the stairs and knocked on the door. There was a long pause and he was just about to try again when the door was opened on its chain.

'Is Ruth there please?'

'She don't live here no more.'

He could just see that it was a young woman and that she was in a dressing gown.

'Do you know where she's gone?'

'Who's there?'

The man started to turn away as he heard the deep voice from inside.

'Some bloke asking for Ruth.'

He had just got to the head of the stairs when a large man wearing a dirty singlet and with tattoos up his massive forearms, wrenched the door open.

'You heard the lady; Ruth ain't 'ere.'

He stumbled down the stairs as the man took a step towards him and could still hear the mocking laugh as he hurried out of the building.

He spent the afternoon wandering around the zoo, trying to make up his mind what to do next and it was while he was in the aquarium that he had the feeling that there was something of significance in the tape recording that he had missed previously. He was unable to put his finger on it, but hurried back to his house and when he found to his relief that there was nobody about played it yet again. The first time round he missed it, but when he put the volume up to maximum, distantly, but quite distinctly, he heard a clock striking. The chime was a most unusual one and it could just have been a grandfather clock, but he didn't think so.

The enquiry agent was extremely expensive, but within forty-eight hours he had found the clock, which was set high up in the tower of a church within a few hundred yards of Knightsbridge tube station. After he had been there himself and listened to it striking from various distances, he was certain that the call could only have come from a fairly small number of buildings, which included a block of flats and about a dozen expensive looking houses.

This time, the enquiry was even more expensive, but within a week he had a neatly typed list of all the inhabitants of the relevant apartments and houses and their occupations, in alphabetical order. Directly he read out the entry to himself, he knew it must be the right girl.

' 'Miss Caroline Ford, aged twenty-one, 24 Wentworth Mansions. Nurse at St Christopher's Hospital.' '

He was able to find out the rest himself; it required care, but within a day or two he had come to the conclusion that there was only one way that a girl from a deprived background could have afforded to live in a flat like that and run a car and that was not just by being a student nurse. The more he thought about it, the more sure was he that she was a prostitute and after another week, the enquiry agent had not only proved it, but was fairly sure that she was operating independently without a pimp.

The man became totally obsessed by

the problem and after long hours of thought, the knowledge that the nurses and for that matter the rest of the staff, were to have anti-'flu vaccines, gave him the idea of how he might dispose of her. He went over the plan time and time again and could see no flaws in his reasoning. No one would suspect that her death was other than due to the 'flu or an unfortunate consequence of the injection and even if he failed to recover the print, there was an excellent chance that he wouldn't be identified from it.

He was only a few paces away from the trolley when the nurse fainted and as he saw the wrong girl about to be injected, he nearly called out, but he hesitated for a fatal second and by then it was too late. The man was seized with a type of madness. He was sorry about the wretched girl who had died, but in an entirely detached way, and even the fact that the police had discovered the cause of death within a few short days did not put him off — next time he would make absolutely certain that nothing went wrong.

* * *

After her breakfast, Caroline felt a lot better, but the 'flu had taken more out of her than she had realized and after having made up the bed with clean sheets, she felt too exhausted to dress and slumped down on to the sofa in the sitting room, listening to a Joan Baez album. She had just begun to doze off, when the front door bell jerked her into full wakefulness. She glanced at the clock on the mantelpiece and saw that it was only eight fifteen; Ingrid wasn't due until the following afternoon and she had made it a rule never to see clients at this flat or without an appointment, let alone at this time of the morning.

She looked through the spy-hole in the front door and saw a man with a thick, black moustache and wearing horn-rimmed spectacles, standing in the corridor. He had on a grey over-all and a peaked cap and was carrying a battered, brown case. Caroline had long since discovered that it didn't pay to be careless and pressed the switch on the intercom.

‘Who is it?’

‘Gas man, madam. There’s a leak been reported on this floor and I’m checking all the appliances.’

‘Just a moment.’

She put on her dressing gown, opened the door and showed him where the cooker and the meter were, then while he was working, she went into the bedroom to put on her make-up. About five minutes later there was a discreet tap on the door and she got up to open it. She failed to see the man immediately and had taken one step outside, when a powerful arm snaked around her neck and simultaneously a mask was pressed firmly over her nose and mouth.

Caroline’s immediate reaction had been to draw in her breath to scream and as a result she inhaled a lungful of the powerful anaesthetic. She just had time to be aware of a burning feeling in her eyes, then all the power went out of her arms and legs and her knees buckled. The man waited for another couple of minutes, then lifted her on to the bed, let a few more drops of the colourless liquid fall from the bottle in his hand on to the lint covering the mask and replaced it firmly over her face.

He took a long time to find a suitable vein, eventually choosing one on the back of her hand, then smoothly inserted the fine needle with its diaphragm attachment. Without hurrying, he then filled three syringes with colourless liquids from three separate ampoules, put a different rubber mask with an attached anaesthetic bag on to the pillow by her head and waited for her to recover consciousness.

The first thing that Caroline became aware of when she came round was the heavy weight on the lower part of her chest, then the fact that she couldn't move either of her arms. As her vision cleared, she recognized the man immediately now that he had removed his hat and glasses.

'You!' she said in a hoarse whisper.

'Yes, it's me and you know what I've come for.'

'This won't do you any good. It's in the bank and if anything happens to me it'll go straight to the police.'

'I don't believe you.' He slowly lifted up one of the syringes. 'Do you know what this is? It's scoline and I've read that it's used as a persuader behind the 'Iron Curtain'; I believe that to be injected with it while still conscious is an experience never to be forgotten. Going to tell me?'

The moment the girl opened her mouth to scream, he pushed an anaesthetic airway firmly in, took her wrist in a vice-like grip and emptied the first syringe into the diaphragm of the needle in the vein on the back of her hand. For a brief moment nothing happened, then the muscles in her eyelids began to twitch and her eyes opened wide with terror.

Caroline felt as if she had been given thousands of electric shocks all over her body. Parts of her muscles kept contracting agonizingly all over her; no sooner did one area relax than it was taken up somewhere else. The pain was appalling and the relief when it finally subsided was succeeded by the horror of finding that she couldn't move. Some saliva trickled down her wind-pipe and she fought desperately to cough, but although every sense was alive, her previously wildly contracting muscles were totally inert. She heard a roaring in her ears, then just when she was on the point of blacking out, she felt a firm pressure over her face and a flow of air forcing itself into her lungs.

The man kept up the artificial respiration until the girl began to breathe spontaneously and watched as she coughed and spluttered, trying to clear the saliva which had been threatening to drown her. He let her recover completely and lifting the second syringe, asked her the same question as before. Her eyes staring and her pupils dilated, Caroline told him about the safe behind the curtain in the kitchen and its combination. With great care, he anaesthetized her again, using the ethyl chloride spray and when she was deeply under, put his thin leather gloves back on and knelt down in front of the safe.

It didn't take him long to complete his search as there was very little inside it, but long enough for his mouth to go dry and his heart to thump as first he failed to find the photograph. He eventually discovered it in the back of a thick address book which was in one of the small drawers and as he stood up and inspected it, he felt as if an enormous load had been lifted from his shoulders. If she really had left it in a bank, he would have been finished and he blessed his instinct that a girl like her would not have trusted it to anyone but herself. She had assured him that this was the only print and that no one else knew about it and such had been her abject terror that he didn't think she had been lying; he was quite certain that only three exposures had been taken originally and he had the other two himself.

The man went back into the bedroom and when the girl began to stir again, he took up his previous position astride her and injected the contents of the third and larger syringe. Within seconds she went flaccid once more and he began to respire her artificially using the rubber bag as a bellows until he was satisfied that all the anaesthetic had been eliminated in her breath. After ten minutes, he took the needle from the back of her hand, removed the mask and massaged her face to remove the marks left by it. He mopped up the tiny drop of blood where the needle had been and saw with satisfaction that not only was there no bruising, but the puncture mark was almost invisible.

Finally, he tucked the girl up carefully in bed, smoothing out her nightdress and the creases in the sheets and blankets and lay her on her side. He knew perfectly well what she must have been going through, totally paralysed and yet fully conscious and slowly suffocating to death, but all of it was essential to his plan of making it look as if she had died from the effects of the 'flu and deliberately, but not entirely successfully, he put it out of his mind. He flung the windows open to disperse the faint smell of the ethyl chloride and by the time he had finished packing his case, the girl's lips were turning blue and two minutes later, she was dead.

Even then, the man did not hurry; he put her slippers neatly under the bed, hung her dressing gown up behind the door and took a last careful look around the flat; only then did he leave.

7

Newton managed to catch George Wainwright before he left his lodgings and it didn't take them long to find out the names of the two girls who had gone to the help of the one who had fainted. If Alison had been right — and the more he thought about it, the more convinced was he that she had — then the girl at risk was most likely to have been the one next in line. Some enquiries at the administrative offices revealed that her name was Caroline Ford and she had not reported for duty the morning after Anne Wilkinson had died; evidently she had telephoned from her flat to say that she had caught the 'flu. Newton had no difficulty in getting her address and phone number and after he had dialled, he listened to the ringing tone for several minutes before replacing the receiver.

'I suppose she could have gone home to her parents.'

'I doubt it,' replied Newton, 'they said at the office that she had nothing to do with them at all. George, I'm more than a bit worried about that girl; obviously she could be on the mend and have gone out to the shops or something, but I think we'd better get round there right away.'

The block of flats was in a quiet street a few hundred yards North of Knightsbridge.

'I thought nurses were always complaining that they were hard up,' said Wainwright as the car drew up outside the main entrance.

'As always, George, you have hit the nail firmly on the conk.'

The front hall was close carpeted and as they stood there looking at the name plates, the porter, wearing a smart grey uniform, came out of the office.

'Can I help you, gentlemen?'

'We've come to see Miss Ford. Do you know if she's in?'

'I haven't seen her go out this morning. I'll give her a ring for you. What name shall I say?'

'Newton. Roger Newton.'

The man came back a few minutes later. 'That's odd,' he said, 'there's no reply. A young lady came to see her the other day and said she was in bed with the 'flu. I asked if she wanted me to send for the doctor, but she assured me that she was getting better.'

Newton held out his warrant card. 'Would you be good enough to let us into her flat, please? We are police officers and I have reason to believe that something may have happened to her.'

The man went back into his office to get the master key and ushered them into the lift.

'Has Miss Ford been here long?'

'Only about six months.'

'Does she have many visitors?'

'Oh no, sir. Very quiet young lady she is.'

The man unlocked the door and Newton put his head round the door. 'Miss Ford!'

* * *

Newton always hated this stage of an enquiry; he and Wainwright had to endure the frustration of waiting while the photographers, the scene of the crime men, the fingerprint experts and Golding, the forensic pathologist, did their work. He watched as the pathologist started his initial examination.

'What's the verdict?' he asked half an hour later.

'Judging by the body temperature, she's been dead between twenty-four and thirty-six hours and there are no external signs of injury at all.' Golding smiled grimly. 'I'm afraid that's all I can tell you at the moment. If our mutual friend's been responsible for this as well, then I'm going to have my work cut out, unless of course he's used the same method again. I'll let you have some further information as soon as I can.'

'Is it possible to be any more precise about the time of death?'

'I'm afraid not; a body under these circumstances, lightly clothed but covered with bedclothes, will reach the temperature of the environment in about twenty-four hours. Rigor mortis usually wears off after about the same time, although it may never develop at all if the conditions are warm. I would be confident that she has been dead for twenty-four hours and certainly not more than forty-eight at the outside. Somewhere between the two is the most likely estimate; I'm sorry, but I can't do any better than that.'

Newton waited until everyone had gone and the body had been removed before discussing it with Wainwright.

'Right, George, let's start in here. I suppose we have to consider the possibility that she died of the 'flu, but that would have to be a very long coincidence and there are other reasons for rejecting that.'

'What reasons?'

'Tell me what strikes you about it first.'

'She was neatly tucked up in bed, no sign of a struggle, slippers under the bed, no suicide note, no empty pill boxes — that's about it I reckon.'

'That's what's worrying me — your first point I mean. It was all far too neat; in the first place, she was lying on her side with her face cradled in her hand

— hardly what I would have expected of someone dying of pneumonia, heart failure or brain infection or whatever else carries off 'flu victims — and secondly, did you notice anything about the bedclothes before they were disturbed?'

'Can't say that I did.'

'Well, the sheets looked quite literally as if they hadn't been slept in, both the top and bottom ones were uncreased and the same applied to the pillow case. See if you can find the dirty ones anywhere; they must have been changed shortly before she died.'

While Wainwright went to look in the bathroom, Newton inspected the built-in wardrobe, which stretched the length of one of the walls. One section of it was locked and eventually he found the key in a carved wooden box also containing some costume jewellery. When he opened the locked door, he found that one part of the area was hanging space and the other a series of drawers, set one above the other. He flicked through the clothes and opened one of the drawers, letting out a low whistle at what he saw.

'George!' he shouted. 'Come in here a moment, will you?'

While he was waiting, he went through the other drawers and took out an object which he brandished at the sergeant as he came in.

'What on earth's that?'

'Your innocence is touching, my dear George. It's what's known in the trade as a dildo. This business is at last beginning to make some sense; our friend Caroline Ford was on the game. Look over here, a school-girl's uniform, a nun's habit, nurse's kit, rubber-wear, leather, even a Polaroid camera.' He lifted up a selection of whips, canes and handcuffs. 'Every taste catered for.'

'I can't see her bringing blokes here, though; she'd have been thrown out in no time flat.'

'I quite agree. My guess is that she went out to work, so to speak. Suppose one of the much respected staff of St Christopher's liked a bit of variety and she either supplied it or got to hear about it? She might even have used this.' He picked up the camera, which still had five unused exposures in it. 'We're getting distinctly warmer, George. This sort of diversion comes pretty expensive and I don't think we need look much further than one of the consultant staff and what's more, one of those who were near the trolley when the vaccines were being done.

'George, I hate to give you all the dirty work, but I want to get back to the hospital. Take this place apart, will you? See if you can find a photograph, a letter or even an address book — this girl must have had contacts. Even if the murderer searched the place himself, he might have missed something. By the way, did you have any luck in the bathroom?'

'I found the sheets, they were in the dirty clothes basket. I also had a quick look in the kitchen and it's quite clear that she had breakfast as her last meal — there was a dirty egg cup, a plate with toast crumbs and traces of marmalade on it and a coffee cup, all neatly stacked on the draining board.'

'Good work, George, that probably means that she was killed yesterday morning, say between eight and nine. Golding seemed quite sure that she had been dead at least twenty-four hours, which gives us the latter time and it is reasonable to suppose that she would have breakfasted at about eight, give or take an hour each way.' He stroked his chin pensively. 'I don't know how the murderer managed to do it without marking her, but it certainly looks as if he put her to bed after killing her; I don't see any other explanation for the clean sheets. There's no reason why he should have gone to all that trouble himself and one can only assume that she changed them herself after getting up that morning. Oh well, I must be off. Good luck with the rest of your search.'

An hour later, Wainwright was beginning to get discouraged; he had finished with the bedroom and was half-way through the sitting room and had found nothing. He had just started on the books in the shelf at the side of the fireplace, when the intercomm sounded.

'It's Stokes here, the hall porter. The Inspector asked me to give you a ring if anyone came enquiring after Miss Ford. That young lady I told you about — the one who's come visiting before — is on her way up.'

'Thanks. She doesn't know I'm here, does she?'

'No, I didn't even speak to her — she's just walked through the hall.'

As soon as the bell went, Wainwright opened the door making sure that the girl wouldn't see him, then as soon as she was right inside, shut it firmly behind her. He saw her eyes open wide with fear and she made a move to get out, but his massive bulk was blocking the way.

'Don't be scared,' he said, 'I'm a police officer.' He held out his warrant card for her to see. 'Sergeant Wainwright, CID.'

'Has anything happened to Caroline?'

The young woman had a slight foreign accent, which he couldn't place but with her very fair colouring he thought she was probably Scandinavian.

'I'm afraid so, she's been killed — murdered.' The girl's hand flew to her mouth and she went pale. 'Why not sit down? Here, let me get you a drink. How about a cup of tea? I could do with one myself.'

Ingrid Andersen smiled in spite of herself — the English and their cups of tea! She was no lover of the police — she had had an unfortunate experience with them once in Paris — but there was something reassuring about this thick-set young man, who, despite his size, did not seem in the least threatening.

'No, let me. I was Caroline's friend, I know where everything is and doing something will help me to get over the shock.'

As she had hoped, he didn't follow her into the kitchen and while the kettle was heating up, she soon had the safe open and directly she found the photograph missing, she quickly stuffed the bundles of notes and the address book into her shopping bag and shut it up again. The one thing she had to ensure at all costs was that she got away before the sergeant either found out her address or took her down to the police station; although she knew that prostitution wasn't actually illegal in England, the police had found ways of harassing some of her friends and if once they got hold of her passport, she would stand a good chance of being deported, which would not suit her at all. She didn't think that Sergeant Wainwright would present too many problems; she knew about men — after all, they had occupied her working hours for five years — and if she was any judge, there was no reason why he should be any less susceptible than all the others.

After she had brought the tea through into the living room, though, she was not so optimistic. The sergeant sat himself firmly down in an upright chair although she gave him plenty of opportunity to share the sofa with her and apart from the odd quick glance at her long, tanned legs, kept his eyes firmly above neck level. If all else failed, she thought, she could always make him an unequivocal offer, but for the moment she decided to bide her time and talk to him.

'May I ask you your name?' he said, pencil poised above his notebook.

'Reinhardt, Ilse Reinhardt.'

'Are you from Germany, then?'

Ingrid's German was more than adequate, certainly good enough to deceive the policeman should he have been able to speak it himself, and she had no hesitation in agreeing.

'Yes, Hamburg.'

'You said you were Caroline's friend. How long had you known her?'

'About eighteen months.'

Ingrid answered the sergeant politely, but always briefly and as a result, he had to make all the running and discovered very little. She knew that they must have found Caroline's gear and had no hesitation in giving him some information about that, particularly as she was enough of a realist to know that pretending to be other than she was wouldn't deceive the sergeant for an instant and if she tried, it would probably only make things more difficult for herself. She was still profoundly shocked by her friend's death, but there was no doubt in her mind that it was connected with the photograph.

Ingrid had only found out about it a couple of days earlier when she had called to see if Caroline was all right. In fact it was only too obvious that the young nurse was the very reverse of all right, indeed she looked extremely ill.

'Don't you think you ought to be in hospital?' Ingrid had said.

'No really, I'd much rather stay where I am; I'll ring them if I'm not better by tomorrow.'

'What about your own doctor?'

'There's nothing much he can do and anyway, I'm sure he's run off his feet.'

As Ingrid turned to go, Caroline, her eyes unnaturally bright, called from the bed.

'Ingrid, if anything should happen to me, I want you to have the money in the safe and anything else you fancy for that matter — the number of the combination is 559142.'

The Swedish girl went back to the bedside and kissed her friend on the forehead.

'Don't be so soft — nothing is going to happen to you. What about some iced lemon — I'll leave a jug for you on the table here.'

Ingrid was getting the ice from the

fridge when she saw the safe, half hidden by a curtain. Although scrupulously honest, she was insatiably curious and she couldn't resist having a look inside to see how much money was there. She found the photograph almost immediately and recognized it at once; not only was Ruth the only person who specialized in that sort of thing, but the position the man had been put in had surprised even her. She also realized the implications of it straight away; there was only one reason why Caroline should have kept it and it upset her profoundly to think that her friend was a blackmailer. She went straight back to the bedroom with the intention of confronting her with the photograph and trying to talk her out of it, but the girl looked so rotten that she hadn't the heart to do it then and she put the print back in the safe.

Ingrid never did get round to tackling Caroline about it. Although the young nurse had improved when she came back to see her the next day, she was still far from well and she put it off again. Inevitably, she speculated about the identity of the man and presumed that he was either someone at the hospital or maybe someone famous. She kept hoping that Caroline might just have taken it from Ruth because it amused her, but that idea was shattered when Wainwright told her that Caroline had been murdered.

She did consider telling the sergeant about the photo, particularly as she could have given him a useful description of the man, but if she did so, she would almost certainly implicate Ruth. Nothing she said now would help Caroline and in a funny sort of way, she had sympathy for the man who was being blackmailed; she reasoned that he wouldn't be a danger to anyone else and so left out all reference to it.

'Have you any idea who might have killed her? I imagine that in your line you can get into some pretty sticky situations.'

'Not if you're careful, and Caroline always was. She never worked without someone being close at hand in case she needed any help and I never heard of her running into any trouble. I'm quite sure, too, that she never brought anyone here.'

'Inspector Newton was wondering if she might have been trying to blackmail someone; we found a Polaroid camera in the bedroom and thought there might be a photograph.'

The sergeant was so close to the mark that Ingrid's first thought was that he had been through the safe before her arrival and was trying to trap her. On reflection, though, she doubted it; her knowledge of combination locks was rudimentary in the extreme, but she didn't think that he could have forced it open so quickly and Caroline was not the sort of person to have left a note of the number lying about. Thinking about the safe suddenly gave her an idea about how she might get away.

'No,' she said slowly, 'I don't think she would have done anything so stupid, but . . . '

'Go on.'

'Well, it may be nothing, but when she was so ill, she told me that she had a safe in the kitchen and that if anything happened to her, I was to . . . but I'm sure you've already looked in it yourself.'

'No, I haven't in fact, I hadn't started on the kitchen before you arrived. Where is it exactly and what about the key? Do you know where she kept it?'

The man's excitement was obvious and Ingrid made a tremendous effort to keep her voice calm.

'It has a combination lock on it and I wrote the number down in my diary.'

She followed him into the kitchen, her shopping bag in her hand, and watched as he knelt down in front of the safe.

'It's rather dark down there. I'll get a torch for you — there's one in the sitting room.'

'Don't bother, thanks. I can manage.'

'It's no trouble.'

Even though he presumed that the fingerprint people had done their stuff, Wainwright manipulated the combination through his handkerchief and moments later, he swung the door open.

'Miss Reinhardt!'

There was something so complete about the silence in the flat, that already the awful suspicion was beginning to creep up on him that he'd made a complete fool of himself. He dashed out into the hall and his suspicions were confirmed; the front door was ajar and there was no sign of the girl. He snatched up the internal phone, but there was a fatal two minute delay before the porter came on the line and in any case, it was a different man.

'No,' he said in response to the sergeant's query, 'I haven't seen anyone, unless you mean the young lady who just went through. Did you want to speak to her, then?'

By the time Wainwright had explained and tried to inject some sense of urgency into the man, who sounded as if he couldn't have hurried whatever the circumstances, the girl had gone beyond recall. He walked gloomily back into the kitchen, picturing what Newton would have to say when he found out.

8

Roger Newton was immediately impressed by Veronica Turner, the casualty staff nurse. She was a good witness, answered succinctly and to the point and like so many red-heads, she blushed easily, a trait which he always found rather touching, particularly as his wife Alison was prone to do the same.

Even though, by now, he was quite sure that Anne Wilkinson's death had been an accident, the detective was still convinced that his best chance of narrowing the field of suspects was to find out exactly what had happened at the time of the fatal injection and although not normally a devotee of the French obsession with reconstruction of crimes, decided that on this occasion it was warranted. He managed to persuade Miss Beale to let him use the same section of the casualty department and was also able to get hold of the girl who had fainted, the one, who with Caroline Ford, had gone to her aid and a couple of others to stand in for Anne Wilkinson and the Home Sister, who was still in bed.

When they had re-enacted the scene several times, even putting out some syringes and with Newton acting Forrester's part, he at last had a really clear idea of exactly what had happened. He dismissed the girls who had made up the numbers and motioned to the others to join him near the trolley.

'Now look, I want all of you to try to remember who else was near the trolley when Patricia here fainted.'

'I'm afraid I can't help,' Patricia replied straight away, 'I've always been scared stiff by injections and I was too busy willing myself not to faint, that I didn't notice anything. No, wait a minute, I remember looking away so as not to see the needle and I'm sure that Dr Poynter was there; I know him well, I work on his ward.'

'Well done; it's amazing what one can remember if one really tries. Now, how about you? Mary, isn't it?' The second girl shook her head. 'Never mind, keep trying.' He smiled in the direction of the staff nurse.

'Well,' she said slowly, 'I'm sure there were at least two others, one a middle-aged man with sandy hair and a moustache whom I didn't recognize, but the other one was Dr Leighton.'

'Professor Raymond was there too.'

'Yes, you're quite right Mary. I'd rather discounted him as he was there on and off the whole time.'

'Why was that?' asked Newton.

'He's the Professor of Microbiology and is in charge of the whole inoculation programme,' replied the staff nurse. 'He also supervised the BCG injections when I was a student.'

'What about the others? I was told that a whole crowd of the senior staff all arrived at about the same time.'

'Yes, that's quite true, but they didn't come near our trolley.'

'I see. Well, thank you all for your help. Miss Turner, there was something else I wanted to ask you if you could spare me another couple of minutes.'

They went back into the office that Newton had been lent and he offered her the easy chair.

'I imagine that there have been a few rumours regarding the reason for us being here.'

The girl smiled. 'You could say that.'

'No doubt some of them have been pretty close to the mark, but nevertheless I'd be grateful if you'd keep this conversation to yourself. The fact is that we're certain that Anne Wilkinson was murdered; a poison was put in her vaccine.'

'But why? And Anne of all people.'

'That's what we've been trying to find out and obviously you can see why it's vitally important to find the person responsible as quickly as possible. I can't tell you the reason at the moment, but I don't think there's any risk of anyone else being attacked; nevertheless, it's impossible to be one hundred per cent certain.'

'You think it was one of the people you were trying to get us to remember?'

'It could have been anyone who had access to the trolley. Do you happen to know any of them? What about Dr Forrester for a start?'

'I can't say I really knew him, but nurses are terrible gossips and I heard quite a bit about him when I was working on the medical wards. He's rather a sad sort of person really; he got a divorce about a year ago and I don't think his career is going very well; he failed the membership for the third time the other day. He was chatting to me about it when we were getting the trolley ready.'

'Did he know Anne Wilkinson?'

'I don't know. He couldn't stand Sister Heywood though.'

'Why not?'

Veronica Turner blushed scarlet. 'He thought that someone like her shouldn't have been in the position of Home Sister.'

'And was he right?'

'Yes.'

'I don't want to embarrass you, but I noticed that you reacted in the same way when you mentioned . . . Who was it?' He consulted his note-book. 'Ah yes, Dr Leighton.'

'You'd think that at my age I'd have

learned not to light up like a beacon at the slightest provocation, wouldn't you? It's just that there was some trouble over a survey that he did a year or two ago and I know a bit about it as I was involved in it in a minor way.'

'Who is he exactly?'

'He's the senior psychologist and he did a study on our intake; it took the form of a detailed questionnaire and some photographs. There was no question of anyone being forced to take part in it if they didn't want to and the purpose of it was fully explained. I know for a fact that several of the girls declined, but of course someone had to complain, and to Sister Heywood of all people. I assumed that what caused all the trouble was the section on our sex lives. It's true that a lot of the questions were pretty direct and I can tell you that I was glad that I was alone when I filled it in, but it was only a small part of the study and, as I said, we weren't compelled to do it. I'm afraid that I don't know all the details, but there was an almighty row.'

'What about the photographs?'

Again came the blush and Newton was not left in much doubt about the type of shots they had been even before she answered.

'Dr Leighton told us that the general build and the degree of maleness or femaleness of the body's configuration and the distribution of hair might be an important clue to the personality, so they took some views of us in the nude, back, front and from either side.'

'Did anyone object to that?'

'One or two, but it wasn't sprung on us or anything like that. In fact, he gave us a lecture on the subject beforehand and showed us some examples — it was very interesting. It was all quite above board, too, the pictures being taken by one of the girls in the photographic department. I couldn't see what all the fuss was about and heaven knows, at that age I was sensitive enough.'

'Who made the complaint?'

'A girl called Anthea Blake — she was one of the Christian Union Brigade.' She saw Newton's half smile. 'I didn't mean to imply that there was anything wrong with Christianity itself, but here, it's riddled with do-gooders and people like Sister Heywood. There was a rumour going around that the girl had been indecently assaulted, but I, for one, didn't believe it; she looked like a boot.'

'How did it all end?'

'It was one of those seven day wonders; most people seemed to think that Dr Poynter stepped in and calmed everyone down.'

'What sort of man is Dr Poynter?'

'He's just about the only character left in the place. I know that some people think he's pompous — Dr Forrester can't stand him — but he's the only consultant here who takes the trouble to involve the nurses, and even the most junior ones, in his ward rounds. He always lets us know what's going on and the patients love him; he's a bit of a bully and likes a bit of ceremony, but at least his rounds are an event and none the worse for that, in my opinion.

'I have personal reasons for being grateful to him too. When I first came here, I got glandular fever quite badly and no one could have been kinder. He was the only person who spotted that I was terrified that I might have leukaemia — my young brother had died of it as a child — and he seemed to know at once that I was too scared to ask.

'He also still does the initial medical examination on all the new intakes of student nurses. I have a friend at St Gregory's and she told me that their examination was quite cursory, but Dr Poynter went to endless trouble over that too; he took nearly an hour over each one and seemed genuinely interested in all of us. The medical students are absolutely terrified of him, but none the less they all try to get on to his firm.'

'I'm also interested in the man with the moustache; he didn't happen to have a pipe in his mouth, did he?'

'As a matter of fact, he did.'

The telephone rang at Newton's elbow. 'Ah, George,' he said, 'and how have you got on?' He listened without making any comment for a long time. 'Hold on a minute, will you?' He shielded the receiver with his hand and looked up at the girl.

'Would you like me to go?'

Newton smiled warmly. 'Would you mind? Thank you so much for all your help. Perhaps I can call on you again if I need any more assistance.'

'Any time you like.'

He waited until she had closed the door behind her and a glint came into his eye.

'George, are you still there? . . . George, you're an ass, more, you're an utter nincompoop.' He listened again. 'Don't be such an idiot, it's not everyone who would have admitted it. Are you free this evening? . . . Good, come round to supper; Alison would like to see you and I want to discuss the case with both of you.'

When he had rung off, Newton looked at his watch and suddenly decided to see Dr Leighton before calling on the Home Sister. The Psychology department was housed on the ground floor of a separate block some distance from the main hospital and he found the man's office without difficulty.

'Come in,' said someone with a loud voice, in response to his knock.

The man who got up from behind the desk was about forty-five and looked as if he would have made a formidable second row forward when he was younger. His massive shoulders threatened to split his ancient corduroy jacket and he gave the detective a broad smile, almost knocking the chair over as he sprang up.

'You must be Inspector Newton; Denis Poynter told me to expect you.'

'That was very prescient of him.'

'He's no fool is Denis, whatever some people may think. He can put two and two together better than the next man, particularly if the next man happens to be me.' He chuckled. 'He told me a couple of days ago that I would be a prime suspect; of course I thought the man was burbling, but it seems that he was right.' Newton confined himself to raising one eyebrow. 'It's true, of course, that I was near the trolley at the time, but so were several others, Denis himself for that matter as well as Raymond and Renfrew. The other thing, though, that seemed to be worrying him was what Sister Heywood might have to say. Do you know, I really believe that that woman is mad. A year or two ago she actually accused me of making a pass at one of her charges; I mean to say, that was a bit rich coming from a dike like her. I was carrying out this investigation, you see, trying to get a detailed psychological profile on one intake of our nurses and then seeing how they turned out later on. If I had been allowed to complete it, it might have revolutionized methods of selecting people for jobs, but Denis thought it would be wiser if I let it drop. I told him that this would look like an admission of guilt, but I bowed to his superior experience.'

'What exactly did Sister Heywood allege?'

'That I had examined one of the girls in an 'intimate' fashion, as she put it. Good God, man, I'm not even medically qualified and she might at least have given me the credit of having some taste — the girl in question would have been enough to have tested the virility of a

Casanova. I was all for taking the bloody woman and her spotty friend to court, but Denis told me to leave it to him, which I did. I can tell you, old man, I stick to monkeys now — much safer.'

'Was that the only reason why Dr Poynter thought that I might suspect you?'

'Why not ask him yourself? It seems a good enough reason to me now; after all, I was there, a young nurse was murdered and I had been accused of interfering with one in the past — I wouldn't have said that that was too bad for starters.'

'Assuming that it wasn't you, would you care to hazard an opinion as to whom it might have been?'

'Come come, Inspector, you can't expect me to be tarred with the same brush as our friend Sister Heywood. If you want theories and better still, accusations, then she's your woman. I'd never even heard of that girl until Denis told me about it, so what use are any opinions of mine?' He got up and went across to a battered looking filing cabinet. 'How about a snort?'

'Not for me, thanks; I have some other people to see.'

'Must be hard work this sleuthing; give me monkeys rather than people any day, nice predictable creatures.'

* * *

'I'm sorry to have to disturb you when you're still ill in bed, but I expect Miss Beale told you why I am in the hospital.'

The woman lying back on the pillows drew her bed-jacket tightly across her chest. Like Forrester, she looked pale and ill and kept taking sips of orange squash to moisten her dry lips and tongue.

'Yes, she said that Anne Wilkinson had been murdered, probably when she had her 'flu injection and that you would be wanting to see me about it.'

Sister Heywood wiped her forehead with her handkerchief and seemed utterly exhausted by the effort of speaking just that one sentence.

'Let me come back tomorrow when you're feeling a bit better.'

'No, it's all right, I want to help you in

any way I can; you see, my whole life during the last twenty-five years has been devoted to the welfare of the nurses here and when I heard what had happened, I was deeply shocked.'

'Would you tell me then what took place around the trolley when the vaccines were given?'

Her account merely confirmed what the others had said. She remembered the order in which the nurses had been in the queue with great accuracy and that Poynter, Raymond and Leighton had been near the trolley at the time — Renfrew she had not seen. The longer that Newton spoke to the Home Sister, the more puzzled he was by her; she had a very faint foreign accent, which he was unable to place, and there was something about her that made him uneasy in a way that he could not define.

'Did you know Anne Wilkinson well?'

'I know all the nurses well — at least all the ones who go through our training school.'

'Was there anything unusual in her life at all?'

'You're wondering why anyone might have wanted to murder her?' Newton nodded. 'I have of course been thinking about that ever since I heard the news.'

The sick woman lay back on the pillows and closed her eyes; when she opened them again a few minutes later, she stared at the detective for a long time as it summing him up and then seemed to come to a decision.

'Dr Poynter came to see me this morning and until he pointed out that I might be a suspect myself, it had never occurred to me that my interest in Anne Wilkinson and for that matter the other student nurses, might be misconstrued.' She saw his puzzled expression. 'Let me try to explain. Do you know what this is?' She pulled up the sleeve of her bed-jacket and on her left forearm Newton saw the crudely tattooed number. 'I see that you do. Perhaps you are already wondering why I didn't have it removed; I'll tell you, I had no right to forget what happened.' She took a deep breath. 'I was born Renate Lang in 1920. My father was a regular army officer and my mother was

English — she was the daughter of a diplomat and they had met before the First World War. My parents never discussed politics with me when I was growing up and like most young people in Germany at that time, I was carried away by the propaganda, the national fervour and the youth programme. I was very blonde in those days and good at athletics and when I was selected to take part in the gymnastics display during the Olympic Games in Berlin when I was sixteen, you will perhaps understand some of my pride.

'My father was in many ways a simple man and after my mother had died in 1938, he positively welcomed the war; he was a professional soldier, his whole training had been directed towards fighting and he had the happiest memories of 1914-18. It was therefore not surprising that not only should I have joined the army nursing service, but that I should have enjoyed the experience as much as he did. I was used to camping, to physical exertion and even now, I look back on my time in North Africa with pleasure. There was still chivalry in that campaign — it was a clean type of warfare and the civilian population hardly came into it.

'I returned to Germany in 1943 and I was at home on leave with my father on the day that was to ruin my life. Colonel von Stauffenberg's attempt on Hitler's life on July 20th 1944 failed and the next day we were arrested. Our house had been used as a meeting place and my father was deeply implicated in the plot; he died a horrible death and I was thrown into a concentration camp.' Sister Heywood took a sip of orange juice and lay back, staring straight in front of herself. 'I can't begin to describe what an impression that that awful place made on me. There was the physical shock of having my hair, of which I was so proud, shaved off and seeing the thousands of women dying of starvation, disease and in the gas chambers; there was also the psychological shock not only of finding out that such places existed, but what my countrymen and women had been doing to the Jews for all those years. It is an excuse that has been used many times that we did not know what was going on, but in my case it was the literal truth.

'At first, I did not want to live, but I found that one's hold on life is stubborn and I did not have the courage to kill myself. The camp doctor must have had his eye on me ever since my arrival, because after a few weeks, I was taken out of the hut and transferred to work in the camp hospital. He had his quarters there and for the next six months, I and another girl were the playthings of him and his friends. A third girl was brave enough to refuse to do what they asked and we had to kneel down and watch while they killed her in front of us — it took them three hours and I still have nightmares about it.

'We were allowed to re-grow our hair, we were kept warm, well fed and clean, but in that time every perversion that you could think of was performed by us and on us. We were also compelled to assist the doctor — if you could give him that title — with his experiments on the other prisoners; we did our best to alleviate their sufferings, but even that has been no comfort to me since.

'As the Allied Forces drew near and the camp officials fled, the other girl and I re-shaved each other's heads, made ourselves as filthy as possible and hid away from the hospital, fearing for our lives at the hands of the other prisoners. When the British Army arrived, because I spoke good English and had relatives over here, I was straight away taken to the RAMC Colonel in charge of the relief work — it was Dr Poynter. It did not take the authorities long to confirm my story that my father had been involved in the plot against Hitler and I was thought to have been a tragic victim of circumstance myself. My friend committed suicide not long after and there were no other witnesses to what had happened; to this day, I have kept the secret to myself.

'I cannot begin to explain the weight of guilt that has been on my shoulders since. I felt guilty as a German, as a nurse who should have found the courage to refuse to assist at those barbarous operations and about all the kindness and consideration I received afterwards — it would have been better for me if I had been kept in prison for ten years. Dr Poynter took endless trouble in arranging for me to go to England and start nursing at this hospital and the sympathy and understanding that everyone showed to me was almost more than I could bear. Perhaps I should have confessed to a priest or a psychiatrist, but I couldn't even find the courage to do that.

'As an individual, I felt physically and psychologically soiled and still do. Before it all happened, I was proud of my body — I had enjoyed skiing and swimming and rejoiced in my ability to please and be pleased by men. After my experiences in the camp, though, it made me physically sick even to think about it. I have been unable to have a close relationship with anyone of either sex since.'

The woman lapsed into silence and Newton was at a total loss to know what to do. There were a number of things he very much wanted to ask her — not least about Caroline Ford — and he was torn between the realization that she would probably tell him more now that the barriers were down and the desire not to upset her further. And so, he sat there quietly and after a minute or two she began to talk again in a flat emotionless voice.

'If it hadn't been for Dr Poynter, I doubt if I would have kept this job, particularly when it came to that business with Dr Leighton. Do you know, this is the first time that I have admitted to myself that most of it was in my imagination? I got it into my head that he was doing that investigation purely for his own perverted ends and that this time I had to stand up and prevent it, whatever it cost me. That poor girl Anthea Blake — I went on at her until she told me the things that I wanted to hear. Dr Poynter calmed it all down — he seemed to understand. I'm ashamed to say it after all the kindness he showed to me, but I even suspected him of showing an unnatural interest in the young nurses.

When I first started my training in Germany, I used to think that doctors were above that sort of thing . . . ' Her voice trailed off and she wiped her forehead again.

'Even my interest in religion was a sham; I thought it might ease my conscience, but it hasn't. I had a chance to be of real help to Anne Wilkinson, but I even made a mess of that. There aren't many causes of morning sickness and I knew at once what her trouble was, but instead of supplying practical help and sympathy, I had to try and find out who was responsible and as a result made things much worse for her. Perhaps it isn't so surprising that my interest in her was misinterpreted and now it's too late to make amends.'

On a sudden impulse, Newton took hold of her hand. Sister Heywood turned her face towards him and with shocking abruptness, her control snapped. The detective had to fight to keep his own emotions in check as the woman broke down and cried as he had never heard anyone cry before, great sobs racking her thin body. It was not until twenty minutes later that she finally quietened down and lay back exhausted, her hair wet with perspiration.

In an entirely spontaneous gesture, Newton gently lifted the back of her hand to his lips.

'It's all over now,' he said softly, 'the past will haunt you no longer; your secret will be safe with me.'

* * *

To say that Newton was quite shattered by his experience would have been a major understatement. He walked straight out of the hospital and strode around for the next hour; he had no idea where his steps were taking him and he didn't care, his thoughts being entirely occupied by the pathetic person in the sick-bay. At first, he couldn't understand why she should have unburdened herself to him of all people, a complete stranger and a policeman at that — but on further reflection he realized that it wasn't so strange after all. He knew, without false modesty, that he was a man to whom people did talk and no doubt, the debilitating effect of the 'flu and the shock of Anne Wilkinson's death had been the last straw for her. Newton had made something of a study of the techniques of interrogation; he was also familiar with the effects of violent abreactions such as Sister Heywood had been through and fervently hoped that the poor woman would now know some peace of mind.

The detective had on a new pair of shoes and the pain in his feet finally forced him to slow down and as he did so, he remembered that he had quite forgotten to warn Alison that Wainwright was coming round that evening. There was a public phone box on the other side of the road and he waited until he had got a proper grip on himself before he rang through.

'Sorry to bounce you like this,' when he had explained the situation, 'I'm afraid that I'll be a bit late myself, too — I've got to see Golding again. Be nice to George, won't you?'

‘What do you mean? I’m always nice to him.’

‘I know, but perhaps you would be especially so tonight; he’s made rather an ass of himself and when I choked him off a bit, he went all guilty on me and offered his resignation. Calm him down a bit, will you? You’re very good at that.’

* * *

‘Are you feeling all right, Roger? You look tired.’

Newton kissed his wife on the forehead. ‘I’m fine, thanks. How’s George? That’s much more important.’

‘A couple of beers and a session playing with Michael have done wonders.’

‘Miracle worker.’

Newton deliberately kept the conversation away from the case until after they had finished supper. In fact, the very last thing he wanted to do was discuss it at all, but on second thoughts realized that this might be the best way for him to come to terms with what had happened that afternoon. He got out his note pad and gave the other two a detailed account of the results of his various interviews.

'Right then, George, it's your turn now; tell us about the glamorous Miss Reinhardt.' He listened in silence until the sergeant had finished. 'Well, it certainly looks as if we guessed correctly about the motive and presumably the murderer removed the evidence from the safe after forcing Caroline Ford to give him the number of the combination, and then killed her.'

'But I thought you told us that Golding had found no evidence of any external injury,' said Alison.

'Yes, that's quite true and for that matter he still isn't certain about the cause of death — he hopes to have the answer tomorrow. He is sure that she was asphyxiated and thinks it was probably done with some sort of anaesthetic; in that case, I suppose, she could have been given some truth drug, but I doubt very much whether in fact they work as well as the fiction writers would have us believe — I must ask Golding when I see him again tomorrow. I suppose that German girl couldn't have got at the safe before you, George, and removed any evidence such as the photo herself?'

Wainwright thought for a few moments. 'The only time she was out of my sight was when she went to make us both a cup of tea, but of course,' he continued gloomily, 'the safe was in the kitchen and she certainly would have had time.'

'What did you find in the safe?'

'The girl's passport, insurance cards — that sort of thing.'

'Any money?'

'About fifty quid.'

'How did that German girl strike you, George?'

'Very pretty, good figure and knew how to use it.'

'I didn't really mean it that way. Did you think she was telling you the truth?'

'Well yes, I did. It seems a funny thing to say about a girl like that, but she struck me as being a very nice person and perfectly straight forward.'

Newton was about to point out that she hadn't been beyond making good her escape extremely skilfully, but judged that

Wainwright was still feeling sensitive about it and decided to hold his peace.

'How did she react when you suggested the possibility of blackmail?'

'She gave me the impression that she hadn't given it a thought, but I suppose she could have known and removed anything incriminating from the safe to use herself.'

'I would have thought that very unlikely. If the murderer was a blackmail victim and had already killed once, I can't see your Miss Reinhardt wanting to run the same risk herself. You've worked on the Vice Squad, George, what do you think are the chances of finding her?'

'It'll take a bit of time, but unless she decides to give up the life and go back to Germany, I think we'll probably get her in the end. While her face was fresh in my memory, I got the photofit people to get out a picture and I've already asked Hemmings to show it to his contacts.'

'You'd better show it to the Aliens' Office and the immigration people as well.'

'I already have.'

'Good man.'

'If only I hadn't let her get away . . . '

'I don't suppose she would have been able to tell us all that much more; anyway, it's no good dwelling on it.' Newton got up and filled Wainwright's glass. 'Now, as far as suspects are concerned, I don't think we need look further than those men around the trolley.' He counted them out on his fingers. 'Forrester, Leighton, Poynter, Raymond and Renfrew.'

'What about the two women?' said Alison. 'Sister Heywood and the staff nurse.'

'I'd rather discounted them. I still think that blackmail's the most likely motive and in addition, I don't see either of them having the necessary expertise; Golding seems to think that Caroline Ford was killed by an intravenous injection of something — he found a minute puncture mark on the back of her hand associated with some bruising.'

'I agree with you about the staff nurse, but what about Sister Heywood? It's not that difficult to give an intravenous injection and from what Leighton and Forrester had to say about her, she sounds as if she is a religious maniac of some sort, as well as being a bit too fond of young women, if the staff nurse is to be believed.'

Newton had dreaded this moment ever since he had left the Home Sister. He was never going to tell anyone what had passed between himself and Sister Heywood that afternoon, not even Alison.

'I think we can rule her out of the second murder on the grounds of timing alone,' he said with an assurance he certainly didn't feel. 'It's quite true that Golding can't fix the time of Caroline's death with any accuracy — he wouldn't commit himself further than about thirty-six hours before he made his initial examination, although he did admit that he could be out by as much as twelve hours either way — but George and I are pretty certain that she had had breakfast on the morning she was killed. People tend to behave in a very stereotyped fashion over things like meal-times, and I think it reasonable to assume that she died between seven and nine a.m. on that day. Sister Heywood was transferred to the hospital from her flat at just before nine a.m. and had telephoned some forty-five minutes earlier.'

'Did she seem really ill to you?'

'Yes, she did and when I glanced at her temperature chart, the readings on it were consistently above 103 degrees right from the time of her admission. I certainly don't think she would have been fit enough to go to Caroline's flat, let alone carry out a complicated murder like that. Another thing, too, several people described her movements at the time that Anne Wilkinson was injected and of all those near to the trolley, she would have had the least opportunity of substituting the syringe.'

'What was her reaction when you told her about Caroline's death?'

'I didn't, and for that matter I haven't told anyone else at the hospital yet. For one thing we still haven't succeeded in tracing her relatives and for another, I didn't think there was anything to be gained by doing so at the moment. I did of course make some enquiries about the girl, but as far as I could judge from having talked to her ward sister and one or two of the others who knew her, she was a quiet person, a good nurse and someone who very much kept herself to herself.'

'Can you eliminate any of the others?'

'Well, I saw Forrester at about twelve thirty on that day and if my guess is correct, he would hardly have had time to get up to London and back — it's a drive of at least two hours each way.'

'What sort of impression did he make on you?' Alison asked.

'Certainly not that of a man who had just driven two hundred miles and murdered a girl. He really did look ill. It's probably not being fair to him, but I had the strong feeling that Sister Heywood might have been on to something about him and Anne Wilkinson; I also thought that that psychiatrist was holding something back. Even if he was responsible for her pregnancy and termination, though, that was no reason for murdering her all that time after.'

'But didn't you think that Anne Wilkinson's death was an accident?'

'Yes, George, I did and still do, but not if Forrester was doing the murdering; he was the one person who could hardly have made a mistake.'

'Have you been able to find any connection between him and Caroline Ford?'

'That's something I'll have to try to look into. He was divorced, but somehow I can't see a young man of his age and in his position wanting to go to a prostitute.'

'Suppose she was his girl friend and he found out that she was one. And don't forget that he might well have been a rapist.'

Newton let out a theatrical groan. 'As the Devil's advocate, Alison my love, you're altogether too efficient. I shudder to think what you'll do to the people I actually suspect; give them cast iron alibis, I shouldn't wonder.'

'Why not try me?' She gave George Wainwright a wink, which Newton intercepted.

'All right, you evil familiar. There are

four others; let's take them in order of seniority. First, Poynter — now he's interesting. My first impression was that he was a bombastic, aggressive little man who drank too much, but clearly several people of entirely different backgrounds such as Renfrew, Leighton, Sister Heywood and Nurse Turner, all thought he had sterling qualities underneath. He's obviously a man who's desperately proud of his achievements, sees his longed-for knighthood slipping away and with his wife having gone into a depression after the death of their child, might have paid for consolation. Any major scandal would clearly destroy him, but he does not strike me as the type to go in for subtle poisoning — by all accounts he has a pretty violent temper. As for Renfrew — I liked him very much.'

'Which means precisely nothing.'

'Which means precisely nothing,' he repeated, giving his wife a little bow. 'He was near the trolley and failed to tell me about it when I first met him, despite the fact that it came up in conversation and indeed I mentioned the precise time when I asked him to find out where that medical student, Simon Buxton, had been. Evidently he is happily married with two sons, one of whom is a student at the hospital. I did discover that he was a specialist anaesthetist when in the RAMC and he would certainly have had the skill and know-how to kill both girls.'

'I still don't see how anyone could have killed Caroline Ford without leaving any marks on her except for that of one injection. It is quite difficult to get a needle into a small vein and she would hardly have waited quietly while he got on with it.'

'I asked Golding that very question and he told me that there were several modern anaesthetics quite capable of rendering people unconscious within a matter of seconds when inhaled through a mask. He has some theory that she was poisoned by an injection after she had been anaesthetized — he gave me all sorts of reasons, but none of them meant anything to me.

'Then we come to Raymond. Not only did he have the easiest access to the botulinus toxin, but, being in charge of the whole operation, was near the trolley the whole time. I've been unable to find out much about him; he's also married with children, seems to be generally liked and certainly dealt with that incident on the golf course with great skill.'

'Surely, though, a man like that wouldn't use a poison that would immediately cause suspicion to be cast on him.'

'I'm not so sure about that, Alison. In the first place, I rang Allenby — he's the other forensic pathologist we use from time to time — and he told me that he didn't think that anyone but Golding would have picked up the cause of death. Although he hates the man's guts, he did say that it was a brilliant piece of work and admitted that he would have missed it himself. Secondly, he might have felt, as you do, that we would hardly suspect him of using stuff out of one of the fridges in his own laboratory.'

'George said that the container had been wiped clean; how many of the suspects were aware at that time that you knew that botulinus toxin had been used?'

Newton thought for a moment. 'That's a good point. Let's see, now, I told Poynter, Renfrew and Raymond myself and Leighton heard from Poynter.'

'That rather lets out Forrester and Sister Heywood then.'

'Yes, I think it probably does.'

'Well then, that leaves Dr Leighton.'

'Yes, Dr Leighton. I didn't take to him at all and I'm more than a little suspicious about that enquiry of his. It's true that he may have been a bit rattled when he was speaking to me, but he made no mention of the photographs, which were obviously one of the sources of complaint.'

'What about the photographs?' said Wainwright. 'If he was doing them to get a cheap thrill, it seems a remarkably obvious way of asking for trouble.'

'I thought they would interest you, George.'

'Come off it, Roger; if I know you, you'd be studying any photographs like that with a magnifying glass if you had half a chance.'

'George, you have a powerful ally there, I'll have to watch what I say. I did in fact ask Golding whether photos would be an appropriate part of an investigation like that and he said they would. He went off on a long spiel about somatotypes; evidently certain personality types are associated with a particular body build and he seemed to think that it was a perfectly legitimate part of a study like that. For that matter, Nurse Turner obviously wasn't worried about it and I must say that Leighton appears to have been quite open about it — he gave all the nurses involved a lecture, saying what he was proposing to do and why.'

'Well,' said Alison, 'I have no wish to be too damping, but you don't seem to have any hard evidence against any of them. What's the next step?'

'Yes, what you say, of course, is quite true and this is where the hard grind will come in. I'll have to check on what they were all doing at the approximate time of Caroline's death and then I'll try to get hold of photographs of those four men and George can ask his Vice Squad friends to hawk them around. There can't be all that many girls who make a thing of photography and it may be our best bet in the long run, although I'm afraid it's going to take an age.'

Alison suddenly got to her feet, her excitement obvious. 'Roger, I've just had an idea about how you might be able to get hold of that Reinhardt girl's address.' The two men looked up at her in surprise. 'She told George that she met Caroline when she was admitted to St Christopher's with virus meningitis about two years ago, right?' Newton nodded. 'Then all you have to do is look up the ward book or diagnostic index and hey presto, you'll get her notes, her address, that of her GP and like enough, her phone number as well.'

'Alison, my love, you're a marvel.' He got up and gave her a hug. 'Now, let's think about the best way to set about it. They're very sticky about patients' notes at hospitals, you know, I've had trouble over them before — confidentiality and all that; they always insist on the patients' permission before divulging any details.'

'Come to think of it, you may not even need the notes; all that information should be in the ward book and that Chief Nursing Officer would probably get it for you. Did she seem a reasonable person?'

'Very. Yes, I think that's an excellent idea. The time I met her, she gave me the strong impression that she would be only too delighted to demonstrate how cooperative the nursing staff would be to highlight Poynter's unpleasant behaviour.'

* * *

As Newton had predicted, Miss Beale was only too pleased to help after he had explained the situation to her over the telephone. By the time he and Wainwright had driven round to her flat in the hospital grounds, she already had the two bulky volumes on the table in the sitting room.

'I was deeply shocked to hear about Caroline Ford, Inspector.'

'Yes, it was a terrible business and we are doing everything in our power to catch the person responsible — I do hope you won't mind if I ask you to keep the information to yourself for the time being.' Miss Beale inclined her head slightly. 'Now, as I said over the phone, we are trying to trace this friend of Caroline.'

'Yes, you said the young woman was in one of the medical wards about two years ago? Well, that shouldn't prove too difficult; Caroline Ford was working on Naylor Ward at that time for a period of about six months, so if you work backwards on that book and I go forwards in this one, we should find the entry all right. You can see how it's laid out, the name of the patient, age, the consultant in charge, home address, GP's address and finally the diagnosis.'

'We think she may well have given us a false name, so perhaps we'd better concentrate on the diagnosis and her age. How old did you think she was, George?'

'Early twenties, certainly no more.'

As it turned out, only two women had been admitted to the ward with a diagnosis of virus meningitis during the time that Caroline Ford was working here and only one of them was in her early twenties.

'This must be the right one,' said Newton. 'Ingrid Johnson, aged twenty-three, 542 Chester Court.'

'That's that big block of flats just off King's Road, isn't it?'

'That's right. We'd better be getting along there, if you'll excuse us Miss Beale; we can't afford to miss this opportunity.'

'Of course. I do hope you find her.'

'Thank you, and also for all your help — I appreciate it very much indeed.'

They shook hands and the two men hurried out to their car.

'Suppose it's the wrong girl or she's moved since those days?'

'Don't be such a prophet of gloom, George. That place is bound to have a night porter and we'll be able to discover straight away if the occupant of flat 542 is the same and with any luck, we should be able to get a description as well.'

9

As soon as Ingrid Andersen left Caroline's flat, she changed the money into travellers' cheques, using several different agencies. She was convinced that if once the police started serious enquiries, it would only be a matter of time before they found her and the right moment to get out was now. It would mean leaving a lot of her clothes and other possessions behind, but the money she had got from the flat would more than make up for that and she valued her freedom a great deal more than a few dresses.

When she got back to her flat, though, she was by no means so sure. She liked London, she was comfortable in this apartment and in any other city, it would take her months to build up the sort of contacts she already had. It was not as if the police knew her real name or would be able to find it out — not now that she had Caroline's address book. She had also been obsessionally careful about this flat and although Caroline had known about it, she was the only one; even Miriam, her agent, only had the phone number. Perhaps, after all, the best thing would be to lie low until either the police found the murderer or all the fuss had died down.

It was a beautiful evening and just before going to bed, she went out on to the balcony to look at the moon. Even with the lights of the city, the stars were magnificent and she went back in to switch off the light so that she could see even better. She was still standing there a quarter of an hour later, when the door bell gave a sharp 'ting'. Immediately, she felt sick with fear; in all the three years she had been there, no one had called on her late in the evening and already she had no doubt that it was the police — they must have found her address in Caroline's flat. She tip-toed across the carpet to the front door, which led straight off the living room. The bell went again and soon after there was a sharp knock and the flap of the letter box was pushed open.

'Miss Johnson! Miss Johnson!'

There was a long pause.

'Can you hear anything, sir?'

'No. This thing won't open very wide, but the curtains must be open; it's quite light in there.'

'What's the next move?'

'Would you nip down and see if the porter has turned up yet and if he has a pass key? I'll stay here just in case she . . .'

The brass flap was released and his voice cut off, but Ingrid was in no doubt that the second man was the sergeant who had talked to her earlier in the day in Caroline's flat. He had a peculiarly deep and resonant voice and she would have recognized it anywhere.

Ingrid was not the sort of person to go into a panic; she hadn't done so in the various crises in her life and she wasn't going to do so now. If she let herself be taken in for questioning, the complications would be endless; at best, she would be deported and she would stand to lose her hard earned savings. But what could she do about it? She knew perfectly well that there were no hiding places in the flat, so went out on to the balcony again and had a careful look round. When she discovered that the French windows would lock on the outside — something she had never noticed before — her first thought was that she might be able to hide out of sight of the windows, the ones flanking the door being so designed that they would only open a few inches, but then she noticed the frosted glass of the bathroom window. She knew for a fact that it would open wide and anyone leaning out would be able to see her on the balcony, wherever she tried to hide herself.

If there was nowhere to hide, then it was only too obvious that she would either have to try to climb out or give herself up. She ran to the edge of the balcony and one quick glance in either direction was enough to rule out the possibility of being able to reach those of the adjacent flats. They were a good fifteen feet apart and the intervening wall was devoid of a ledge or indeed of any other hand or foot-hold.

Feeling sick with apprehension, she looked down at the pavement a good fifty feet below and was overcome by a spasm of vertigo. The prospect above her was not a lot better; although the concrete floor of the balcony above was only about eight feet above her head and if she stood on the iron balustrade, she would undoubtedly be able to reach it with ease, she was no sort of gymnast and without a ladder, she knew she would never be able to make the climb. One of her nylon sheets would obviously help her to make the ascent if she knotted it at intervals and the ironwork was in good condition, but would she have the nerve to use it? She hung out over the edge as far as she could; climbing down would without doubt be much easier and if she doubled up the sheet, making it into a loop, it would not only give her a firm foothold, but if once she got down she undid the knot, she would be able to pull it down after her.

It did not take Ingrid long to make up

her mind; her fear of the police was even greater than that of the climb. She went into the bedroom and put her passport, precious address book, travellers' cheques and her few pieces of good jewellery into a shoulder bag, took a clean nylon sheet out of the airing cupboard and then locked herself on to the balcony. She had just turned the key when she suddenly remembered that she had left the chain on the front door. Forcing herself not to hurry, she crept back inside, slid the end of the chain out of the metal channel and went out once again. Any minute, she expected to see the room behind her flooded with light and she quickly threaded the sheet through the lowest rung of the balustrade and tied the two ends together. It hung down in a loop about three feet long and before her nerve failed, she stepped over the edge with her back to the awesome drop and reached down with her right leg. Holding on to the concrete base with both hands, she gradually put her full weight on to the bottom of the loop, then transferred her grip to the sheet and extended her left leg as far as it would go. Her toes found the top of the balustrade below and within a few more moments, she was standing safely on the balcony.

It was essential to her plan to retrieve the sheet, but the knot had pulled tight and she tore at it with her fingers, her arms aching with the effort of working above her head. At long last it came loose and, with a sob of relief, she pulled it down and sat on the concrete to regain her breath.

There were about a thousand flats in the block and apart from the people on either side of her, with whom she was on nodding acquaintance, she knew no one and thus had no idea on whose balcony she was sitting. The French windows behind her were locked and the curtains drawn and she was just trying to think what she was going to do next, when the light came on above and soon after she heard the bathroom window being opened.

'What's it like?'

'Sheer drop. Not a chance of anyone getting down here.'

The window was slammed shut and Ingrid breathed a sigh of relief; the first hurdle was over. With the help of the sheet, she thought she would probably be able to climb back up, even though it would be much more dangerous and difficult than the descent, but to have gone to all this trouble, the police must want her very badly and it seemed quite likely to her that they would leave a watch on the flat all night and even for several days. That left her with the choice of staying where she was or climbing right down to the street. It took her five minutes to screw up enough courage to start for the floor below. She made it, but only just; the knot slipped as she was stepping down and only a frantic grab at the balustrade prevented her from hurtling to the ground, forty feet below. She just managed to save her precious sheet, but there had been an ominous clang as her shoe caught the ironwork and she stood there petrified, expecting a light to come on in the room behind her at any minute.

She waited for five minutes, massaging her bruised leg and trying to work out what to do next. Light was streaming out of the flat immediately below and she could hear music coming softly through the open French window. Although the thought of stepping over the edge again filled her with horror, she waited for a full half hour hoping that the person below would go to bed, but the music continued and when she leaned over the balustrade, she saw the glow of a cigarette and shrank back again.

Ingrid tried the door behind her without any expectation that it would be unlocked and gave a gasp of surprise when it opened. She hesitated for a long time before deciding to go through the flat behind her, but in the end decided that anything was better than to have to face a further climb. She was certain that the lay-out of the apartment would be exactly the same as hers and she was further encouraged by the complete silence from inside.

During the time she had been waiting outside, it had clouded over and even though she opened the curtains a few inches when she was right inside, it remained pitch black. She stood there immobile for a few more minutes and as her eyes became adjusted to the gloom, she could just make out the door. All went well until she was half-way across the room, when her toe caught in something on the carpet. Out of the corner of her eye, she saw a dark shape beginning to tilt and made a frantic grab for it; her finger tips just brushed it and then the table lamp fell on its side with a tremendous crash, its china base breaking into fragments.

There was a cry of alarm from within the bedroom.

'Who's there?' The quavery voice was high pitched with approaching hysteria.

Ingrid was half-way down the first flight of stairs before the screaming began and the sounds gradually receded into the distance as she took the steps three at a time. Something made her hesitate before turning the corner into the large entrance hall and she put her head round cautiously, withdrawing it abruptly as she saw the thick-set man, who had policeman written all over him, who was talking to the porter.

At night, all the other exits to the block of flats were locked and she waited there, shivering with reaction. A man in a dressing gown emerged from the lift and began to talk excitedly, gesticulating wildly and in response to a sharp command from the plain clothes man who ran to the door, two policemen in uniform came hurrying in from outside. She stayed there until they had gone up in the lift, hoping that she would be able to slip out of the building, but the porter never moved from his position in the hall. She had often come in late and knew that particular man quite well; she was absolutely certain that he would have been warned to keep an eye out for her and she went into the ladies' cloakroom and locked herself into one of the cubicles.

* * *

Paul Harrington had overslept, was late for the office and to cap everything, the rain was coming down steadily. He hesitated at one of the side doors of Chester Court and then turned, preparatory to making his way to the front exit; there was a taxi rank right outside, but in the rain, and if his usual ill-luck persisted, he guessed it would be empty.

'May I share your umbrella?'

Harrington's face lit up as he saw the extremely attractive blonde girl, who was standing only a few feet away — to hell with the rain and being late for the office.

'It isn't a very large one,' he said as he shook it out.

The girl smiled and gave him a look that spoke volumes.

PC Forbes tried unsuccessfully to shelter from the rain on the opposite side of the street and stamped his feet, attempting to warm them up; his boots leaked and he was feeling thoroughly fed up. It didn't improve his temper either to see the young couple who had just come out of the side door; their faces were hidden beneath a black umbrella, but as they went by, he saw the girl put her arm around the man's waist and pull him closer to her.

'All right for some,' he said to himself irritably and began to pace up and down once more.

* * *

Newton was in a thoroughly bad mood when he got up the following morning. He had been so sure that they were going to find the girl and then had come the disappointment of discovering that the flat was empty, but that was nothing compared to his anger when Wainwright had rung him in the small hours. The coincidence of a burglar being in the flat two floors directly below had immediately seemed too much to accept and the finding of the crumpled sheet, which matched the others on the bed, out on the balcony had clinched it. The block of flats was like a rabbit warren and he was quite certain, straight away, that the girl had escaped yet again. He also had the feeling that someone of such obvious courage and resource would be very difficult to find and what made it worse was his intuition that for her to have gone to such lengths to get away meant that she knew something important. After the phone call, it took him hours to get off to sleep again and when eventually he did so, it seemed only minutes before the alarm went off.

The sight of Golding's face did nothing to improve either his temper or the splitting headache which was hammering away at his temples. The pathologist was obviously bubbling over with excitement and his attempts to retain his habitually lugubrious expression were a complete failure. He rubbed his hands together as the detective came into his office and waved him into a chair.

'You've got a real expert at work here,' he said, 'it's a pleasure to pit one's wits against him. I was looking for a subject to present in a paper to the meeting of forensic pathologists in New York early next year and this will do very nicely, very nicely indeed.' He went across to the book-shelf, took down a volume and read the title of an article in French with an accent that would have made Sir Winston Churchill sound like a member of the Académie française. '*Leçons sur les effets des substances toxiques et médicamenteuses, par Claude Bernard*.'

Newton, who spoke French well and loved the language, couldn't stand it any longer when Golding opened the book at a marked page and began to read again.

'My French is a bit rusty, do you think perhaps . . . '

The pathologist turned with a self-satisfied smirk on his face. 'My dear chap, thoughtless of me. Now, let me see . . . 'Within the still body and staring death-like eyes, feeling and intelligence persist strongly. His consciousness persists whilst his organs die one by one imprisoned within a cadaver . . . The torture that existed only in the minds of poets is produced by the nature of the action of the South American poison.' '

'Curare?'

Golding closed the book with a loud snap. 'Precisely. There were, however, some very odd features to this case; the pharmacology people found quite a high concentration of the drug in the urine and it is most unusual for it to appear there in under five minutes. In my view the dose given to this girl would have proved fatal in about two minutes, unless of course she was artificially respired for some time.'

'If you are right, why on earth would the murderer want to do that?'

'I suppose it could have been a sadistic desire to make her end as unpleasant as possible, but it could also have been done to eliminate any traces of an anaesthetic he had used earlier; some of them are very volatile and are eliminated in the expired air. At any rate, although we looked most carefully, we found no traces of the commonly used ones in her body.'

'What makes you so sure that she was anaesthetized?'

'There were no signs of violence at all. Something must have been used to render her unconscious within seconds; several anaesthetic gases will do this, but to have the same effect, an injection would have to have been given intravenously and no one could have achieved that without causing bruising and as you already know, I found only one minute puncture mark on the back of her hand, which was probably where the curare was administered after she had been anaesthetized.'

'So you think her death would have been rather like that of Anne Wilkinson?'

'I'm afraid so. I pity those two young women, I really do.'

'But why should the murderer have gone to such lengths?'

'Well, with just a little bit more luck, the death of those two girls would have been put down to the 'flu.'

'In fact, if anyone but you had done the autopsies.'

'My dear Inspector, you are too kind.'

'Would anyone but an anaesthetist have had the skill to have done all this?'

'I don't really see why not — the technical side wouldn't have been all that difficult.'

* * *

Newton walked back to his office at the Yard and found Wainwright waiting for him.

'What are you looking so pleased about, George?' he said. 'I would have thought that last night would have been enough to dampen your spirits permanently.'

'That girl did go to the safe while she was making the tea.'

'Tell me more.'

'Well, I took the teapot along to Mitchell so that we could send copies of her prints around Europe and I suddenly thought that she might also have left them on the safe, and she had — not only on the handle, but inside as well.'

'And you said there was still some money left inside?'

'Yes, about fifty pounds.'

'I bet you she was looking for evidence that she knew had been inside the safe. The important questions are, what was it and did she find it?'

'Perhaps the murderer got there first?'

'Perhaps he did,' Newton said slowly. 'George, you've given me an idea — what was the number of that combination lock?'

Wainwright consulted his notebook. '559142.'

Newton wrote it down and studied it for a few minutes. 'If ever you use one of these don't use your birthday — you'd be surprised at the number of people who do.'

'How do you mean?'

He held up the notes he had made on Caroline Ford. 'She was born on the second of April, 1955 — she just had the digits reversed. Excuse me a moment.' He picked up the outside telephone. 'Get me Mr Styles at St Christopher's Hospital, would you please? . . . He's the senior administrator.' The operator rang back within a few minutes. 'Mr Styles? . . . Good morning, Inspector Newton here. Are the medical staff due to have a meeting in the near future? . . . Next Monday? Admirable. And how many are likely to attend? . . . What about the non-medical people like Colonel Renfrew and Dr Leighton? . . . Splendid. Perhaps I could see you on Monday? About two p.m. suit you? . . . Good, thank you very much. Goodbye.'

'What was all that about?'

'Just an idea I'm proposing to put to the test on Monday. Look, George, keep after that Johnson girl, will you? But will you be sure to be back here by five p.m. on Monday? Hang around until I give you a call.'

10

Roger Newton felt all the better for the weekend he spent away from work; he played a couple of rounds of golf with his father-in-law, went to the Country Club dance with Alison and best of all, had escaped from the tyranny of the telephone for a full forty-eight hours.

On the following Monday morning, he cleared up some outstanding items of work and promptly at two p.m. was shown into Styles' office.

'What can I do for you?' the hospital secretary asked after they had sat down.

'This meeting the staff are having at five o'clock — what's it about?'

'We're on the point of launching a public appeal for the medical school and the representative of the firm that's organizing it is coming to discuss the plans.'

'So that's why you expect everyone to be there?'

'Yes, that's right. All the senior members of staff have been asked to sign deeds of covenant; it looks much better when the City and the charitable trusts are being approached if it can be shown that the staff have already made a substantial contribution.'

'And have they?'

'Oh yes. There have been a few exceptions, but not many.'

'I'd very much like to see and hear what goes on at that meeting without being observed myself.'

The secretary frowned. 'I don't know about that, you see . . . '

'I wouldn't have asked if it hadn't been of vital importance and of course I wouldn't expect you to take any responsibility if my presence was discovered. I would only need to be there for a few minutes at the very outside.'

'There's nothing confidential about the meeting, but . . . '

'Splendid,' said Newton decisively. 'Perhaps I could take a look at the room?'

Styles had no idea what to do; on the one hand he wanted to cooperate with the police and on the other, knew exactly what Poynter would say if he ever found out. He was still far from confident in his job and would dearly have liked to ring up his superior at the Area Health Authority, but almost before he knew what he was doing, they were in the board-room and he found himself discussing, not whether the Inspector should be there at all, but where he was going to hide. He only really began to recover his equanimity when it became obvious that there was nowhere. There was only one entrance, a pair of doors that opened off the front hall of the hospital, and the windows, all of which were at the other end, looked out on to a courtyard some twenty feet below.

'It doesn't look very promising I'm afraid; I suppose I could ask Dr Poynter if you could sit in on the meeting.'

Newton didn't reply for a moment. 'That's not really quite what I had in mind,' he said eventually after having taken one last look around the room. 'Perhaps I'd better leave it after all. I'd be glad, though, if you'd keep the fact that I was enquiring to yourself.'

Styles breathed a sigh of relief and after a few polite enquiries about the progress of the case, left the Inspector in the front hall. Newton watched the man disappear into his office and paced up and down, deep in thought, until the sight of Brookes, the head porter, gave him an idea. Alison had told him that in most hospitals the man in that position knew more about what was going on than anyone else and he had made a point of introducing himself during the previous week.

'Your board-room's a very interesting old place, Mr Brookes.'

The man smiled. 'Yes, it was used as a chapel in the last century.'

'I was wondering about that with all that stained glass.'

'Very valuable it is too; they took it all out and stored it somewhere safe during the war.'

'What about the gallery above the door?'

'That's the old organ loft.'

'Is the instrument still up there?'

'Yes, as a matter of fact it is.'

'Would it be possible for me to take a look at it? I'm very interested in old organs.'

The old man looked a bit doubtful, but the beers that George Wainwright had plied him with at the local pub on the first evening they had been there, had not been wasted.

'You won't tell anyone you've been, will you sir? Two of the students went up there last year and started to play it during a meeting and ever since then I've had strict instructions to keep it locked up.'

The entrance to the gallery was up a steep flight of stairs leading off a passage-way at the side of the board-room and it was obvious as soon as the detective climbed up that it would be an ideal place for him to watch the meeting without being observed and he blessed his luck that Styles had neither appeared to have noticed it nor even been aware of its presence.

The organ was in fact an instrument almost totally without merit and was covered in dust and cob-webs. Newton moved a few rotting hassocks and a pile of hymnals to make sure that he would be able to move about silently, tested the floorboards and after a decent interval returned the key to the porter's lodge. Fortunately for him, a new Yale lock had been fitted and he was able to leave the door on the latch, jamming it at the bottom with a spent match with sufficient firmness to prevent it from being opened by a casual push or a gust of air.

When Newton returned at 5.30, he went straight to the administrative offices across the hall from the board-room.

'Is Mr Styles in?' he asked the secretary, who was looking through a bulky file.

'I'm afraid not, Inspector. He's attending that meeting in the board-room.'

'I wonder if you'd help me then? I particularly want to get these notes to four members of the staff rather urgently — it can't wait until the end of the meeting, I'm afraid.'

The girl smiled. 'Leave it to me. I'm looking up something for Mr Styles at the moment and I've got to go in there anyway. I'll be a few minutes, though; will that be all right?'

It couldn't have suited Newton better. Long before the girl went into the board-room, the detective was up in the gallery behind the wooden screen, which partially hid the organ. A rectangle had been cut in it, presumably to allow the organist to see the altar and through it, he had a clear view of the room. There must have been some eighty men and women there, with about half of them sitting round the series of tables which had been placed together in the centre of the room and the remainder on chairs against the walls. Both Poynter and Renfrew were at the far end of the table, Raymond was half-way down one side and Leighton was sitting with his back to the left hand wall.

Newton had brought a pair of binoculars with him and studied the four carefully while they listened to the fund-raising expert, who was now in full spate. Poynter, as befitted the chairman, was looking up at the speaker and listening intently, while Renfrew was puffing away at his pipe and contemplating the row of portraits along the wall to his left. The remaining two men were otherwise occupied; Raymond was drawing a complicated doodle on the edge of his agenda and Leighton was doing the *Times*' crossword with the help of one of his neighbours.

The effect of Newton's notes to the four men could hardly have been more of an anti-climax. The girl came in and handed them to Styles and the detective watched carefully as they were passed round. Each message was identical; he had written down the number of the combination lock of Caroline Ford's safe and asked them to leave a message for him in the porters' lodge after the meeting if it meant anything to them.

Poynter and Renfrew, who were sitting nearest to Styles, received theirs almost simultaneously. Poynter gave his only the most casual of glances, then stuffed it into his pocket and went on listening to the speaker with rapt attention, while Renfrew read his carefully and then scribbled a few words on it with a pencil. Raymond also read his carefully, frowned and then folded it neatly, put it under the pile of papers in front of him and continued with his meticulous drawing. Leighton was the last to receive the message; Newton saw his face twist into a smile, he made an aside to the man sitting next to him and after a moment or two filled in the answer to another clue.

Newton watched for another twenty minutes and then crept back down the stairs, pulling the door to behind him. He wandered into the quiet court-yard opposite the main entrance to the hospital and sat down on a bench, contemplating a sparrow which was having a dust bath on the path a few feet away. He had been so convinced that one of the four men was the murderer, but now his confidence was severely shaken. He had watched them all carefully through his binoculars both at the time they had received the notes and at intervals over the ensuing twenty minutes and not one of them had reacted with the least show of guilt.

He got up and for the next hour walked

around the neighbourhood, going over all the evidence again and reconsidering all the suspects. At the end of it all, he was forced to the conclusion that unless the murderer made another move or there had been a photograph and they were able to locate it through the missing girl, their chances of catching him or her would be very small indeed. He had very little faith that their other enquiries with the vice squad would lead anywhere and was becoming progressively more depressed by the whole affair.

The clock on the church at the other end of the square was striking seven as Newton approached the hospital again and he saw Brookes standing on the steps.

'I was hoping to see you, sir; these two notes were left for you about half an hour ago.'

One of them was just his original note, folded over and with a pencilled comment on it. 'Sorry, it doesn't mean a thing. A.R.' He looked at the envelope with more interest; it was addressed to him in a scrawly handwriting, with URGENT written across the upper left hand corner.

'Did you happen to see who left either of them?'

'No, sir. Everyone came out of the meeting at the same time and I found them lying on the counter after they had passed through the hall.'

Newton thanked the man and opened the brown envelope with his pocket knife. The note, written on a sheet of hospital note-paper, was short and to the point: 'May I see you? 7.30 p.m. in my laboratory? Clive Leighton.'

Newton glanced at his watch and then put through a call to Wainwright at the Yard.

'Ah, George, would you mind hanging on there until I ring back — I'm just off to see Leighton and I have a feeling that this is it.'

'In fact, he rang here asking for you about twenty minutes ago and I told him I thought you were still at the hospital. How long will you be?'

'Difficult to say, but lay on a car, will you please, just in case?'

'Then you think he's our man, do you?'

'It's beginning to look like it.'

* * *

The psychology laboratories were in a separate block some two hundred yards from the main buildings. At that time of evening, there was no one about and Newton went straight to Leighton's office and knocked on the door. When there was no reply, he tried again and finally turned the handle and pushed. The door was locked and he hammered on it again.

'Dr Leighton! Dr Leighton!'

Newton waited for several minutes, then turned and started to walk slowly along the corridor. He was unable to locate the light switch and in the gloom had to pick his way carefully to avoid the broken bits of apparatus, filing cabinets and old magazines which were piled high against the walls. He called out once more and then began to try the other doors on both sides. The first two were also locked, but he saw a faint light coming from under the third and it came open as he pushed. He was momentarily blinded when he looked in, but then started forward as he saw the dark shape on the floor covered by a blanket except for the white rubber boots, which were protruding from one end.

Newton ran across the room and in the same moment that he ripped back the blanket and saw the pile of old journals, the door came to with a muffled thud and he heard the key turn in the lock. The detective straightened slowly and walked backwards towards it; he gave it a few experimental thumps with his fist, but it was immediately obvious that he would be unable to make any impression on it. There was no handle on the inside, the whole thing fitted extremely tightly and when he lay with his back on the floor and kicked it hard with the sole of his shoe, it felt totally unyielding.

Apart from the magazines, the blanket and the rubber boots, the room was quite empty and with the all-pervading smell, Newton could only assume that it was some sort of animal house. There were no windows, the powerful bulb in the ceiling was protected by thick, unbreakable glass and all the walls were white-washed. The room was rectangular, about twenty feet by twelve and apart from the ventilator grilles, the only other feature was a large mirror set into the centre of the wall to the right of the door.

The detective's immediate reaction had been that Leighton was playing some childish practical joke on him, but even so, after only a few minutes, he began to feel the panic threatening to break out. Ever since he had been shut up in a concrete bunker and left to suffocate by the murderess, June Fordham, some three years earlier, he had been troubled by claustrophobia and although he forced himself to go into lifts on his own, it was always an effort and he knew that if he was compelled to spend the night shut up in this room, something was going to snap.

He felt the sweat beginning to break out on his forehead and to take his mind off the situation, inspected the door even more carefully. The first thing he discovered — and that was a great consolation in view of his previous experience — was that there was a little air coming in beneath it; it wasn't much, but enough, he was sure, to keep him going. It was, though, very soon clear that cutting any sort of hole through it with his flimsy pocket knife would be beyond him; it only had one blade and that was blunt.

Moving away from the door, he knelt down to examine the ventilation grille and at that moment, the light went out. The feeling of impending suffocation was ten times worse in the dark and he clenched his fists, hurting the palms of his hands with his finger nails in an attempt to prevent himself from screaming. Taking deep breaths, he forced himself to relax and felt for the light switch. It took him some time to find the door again, so closely did it fit into the wall, and when he did, it did not take him long to discover that there wasn't a light switch there, or anywhere else for that matter. He made an effort to see the room again in his mind's eye and now remembered that a peculiarity of the room was that the light in the centre of the ceiling was the only thing that projected into it, the door, the mirror and the ventilator grilles being flush with the plastering.

When he had been near the ventilator grille, Newton had thought that there was a faintly ether like smell; now, he was quite sure of it. He felt his way back and the suspicion that some form of toxic gas was coming down the shaft became a certainty; not only could he feel the movement of air down there, but when he took a cautious sniff, not only did his eyes begin to prick, but almost immediately he developed a sensation of unreality and light headedness. He felt his panic beginning to subside and drifted into a day-dream, imagining himself back at home with Alison and the baby. He gave a sudden cough and it was enough to break the spell; he crawled away across the room, stood up against the far wall and immediately began to feel more himself. The temptation to give in and sink into oblivion was still almost overwhelming, but as the moments went by, his mind cleared even further and he began to think constructively once more.

Newton knew very little about anaesthetic gases, but moistened his handkerchief with saliva and tied it round his mouth and nose in the hope that this would afford him some protection. Whatever type of gas it was, it seemed to be heavier than air and extremely potent and he had a feeling of utter despair, knowing that he would be unconscious within minutes and like enough, dead shortly after that.

He was quite determined that at least his colleagues should know what had happened to him, so he began to write down an account in his note-book. He had only just started, when for no reason that he could explain, he suddenly found himself thinking about the mirror. There was the animal smell, the lack of furniture, the fact that there was no light switch and Leighton being a behavioural psychologist; surely this all pointed to it being a two-way one.

He hurried across to the wall in which it was set, found the mirror without difficulty and gave it a sharp blow with the butt of his hand. There was no doubt that it gave ever so slightly and without pause for further thought, he pulled off his shoe, gripped it by the toe and swung at the glass with every ounce of his strength. There was a tinkling crash and with a few more feverish blows, the detective knocked out the rest of it and clambered through the opening left in the wall and blundered around the room trying to find the light switch.

There were a series of resounding crashes as he knocked into pieces of apparatus which seemed to be everywhere, but finally he found it and the room was flooded with light. Within seconds he had turned off the two orange gas cylinders, which were connected to the ventilation system by lengths of plastic tubing, and switched on the air conditioning. Newton staggered across to the window and the blind went up with a crash as he tugged on the cord; then he had the window open and leaning out as far as the metal bars would allow, he sucked in great breaths of fresh air. Gradually his intense feelings of nausea subsided and within five minutes he was almost back to normal with only a slight headache to remind him of his ordeal.

One quick look out of the window was

enough to satisfy him that there was no hope of getting out that way; all of them on the ground floor of that particular block were protected in the same way, heavy iron bars being set into the brick-work of the surround. Now that he had a chance to look at the room more closely, he was horrified to see how much damage he had done; two cameras, one a still and one a ciné, had been knocked over on their tripods and an expensive looking tape recorder was lying upside down on the floor. When he came to lift it up, he found that it must have weighed all of forty pounds and yet he had no recollection of having hit anything as bulky as that. As he straightened up and put it back on the table, he noticed something lying on the ground nearby amongst the glass from the two-way mirror. He lifted it up, smelled it and then put it carefully into one of the envelopes lying on the desk. Only then did he give his attention to the door; it was of solid construction and even though he found a tool box containing several screw drivers in a cupboard, it took him nearly half an hour to get out.

It was only when he went into the cloakroom in the front hall of the main hospital building that Newton realized what a mess he was in; the knee of his left trouser leg was split and under it there was a deep cut in his thigh. The gas from the orange cylinders must have had some pain relieving qualities because only now was he beginning to feel the pain from it and the enormous bruise which was already discolouring his right thigh and which must have been caused when he knocked the tape recorder off the table. He was still feeling faintly nauseated and the face that looked back at him from the mirror would have looked perfectly well at home on one of Golding's mortuary slabs.

Newton limped across to the lodge and the porter soon got through to the Yard for him.

'George,' he said, 'come round to the hospital right away, will you? You'd better bring a couple of men with you.'

'O.K. Be with you in fifteen minutes.'

'There's no need to hurry; give me half an hour, will you? I'll meet you outside the front entrance.'

To Newton's relief, Nurse Turner was on duty in the casualty department, which saved him a lot of difficult explanations. She put a dressing on his knee, got one of the other nurses to sew up the tear in his trousers and sponge away the worst of the blood, and a cup of tea completed his revival.

'That was a real life saver,' he said when he had finished. 'Tell me, do you know anything about anaesthetic cylinders?'

'Not much, I'm afraid. What did you want to know?'

'I was anxious to identify a bright orange one.'

The girl shook her head. 'It doesn't ring a bell with me, but I tell you what, I'll ask the anaesthetic SHO; he's down here helping with the reduction of a fracture and they're not quite ready yet.'

'Don't you worry, tell me where he is and I'll go and ask him myself.'

'Not without your trousers, you won't,'

she said, laughing and trying unsuccessfully to stop herself from blushing. 'I'll bring him over. Anyway, I think you ought to sit there quietly for a bit, that fall has upset you more than you realize — you're still as white as a sheet.'

The detective realized how right she was, when the girl had gone and was glad to be able to lie back for a few minutes; it was a relief that she had believed his story of a fall and he was feeling a lot better when the anaesthetist arrived. The young man listened to Newton's description and nodded his head.

'Cyclopropane,' he said without hesitation. 'We don't use it much now.'

'Why not?'

'Because it's both expensive and highly explosive.'

'Is it now? Can you tell me anything else about it?'

'It acts extremely quickly and is very good for casualty work, particularly for things like fractures when there is no need for the diathermy. It's possible to induce people within a matter of seconds and it's pretty safe from an anaesthetic point of view. Now, let's see, what else? It's heavier than air and has an ethery sort of smell — that's about it, I think.'

'What happens if the concentration builds up?'

'The patient gets more and more deeply unconscious until eventually he stops breathing. The gas is pretty safe because you can get good anaesthesia well short of the danger level.'

'Is it still in use?'

'Oh, yes. There isn't a cylinder down here, but I know there are some up in the theatre.'

'Are they kept locked up?'

'Good gracious no.'

* * *

By the time that Newton's trousers were ready, the half hour was up and the police car was already parked outside.

'Are you all right, sir? You look a bit rough.'

'Come inside, George, and I'll tell you about it.'

The two men went into the office they had been lent and the detective gave Wainwright a full description of what had happened.

'And so, you see, I was bloody lucky to get out of there alive and for that matter not to have caused an explosion — one good spark produced when I was chiselling around the lock to get that door open, would have been enough to send the place up.'

'What are you going to do now?'

'Well, I have a shrewd idea who our murderer is, but I haven't a shred of hard evidence and we'll just have to hope that he cracks when we set up a confrontation. George, I want you to ring up each of those four men, Poynter, Renfrew, Raymond and Leighton, and get them to come here somehow. Use any excuse you can think of, but for God's sake don't let them know that I'm here. Our murderer must think I'm dead and he's going to get the shock of his life when I do my Lazarus act.'

Wainwright let out a theatrical groan.

'That's a pretty tall order, sir; what am I going to say?'

Newton thought for a few moments. 'You could say that I've disappeared and that there's been another murder — that should bring them running and I imagine that the guilty one won't want to show too much reluctance.'

'Which one of them do you think it is?'

'I'm sorry, George, but I'll have to keep you on tenterhooks a bit longer; you see, I don't want our man to have any suspicions that we know about him and although I realize that you are the Henry Irving of the Force, it would be very easy for you to put him on his guard if I told you now.'

'Henry Irving, sir? I don't get it.'

'Skip it, George. Pick up that phone, will you?'

Wainwright put on a much better performance than Newton had expected. He managed to keep it short enough to prevent them from asking too many questions, but gave enough detail to intrigue them. Predictably, Poynter made the most fuss, but by a piece of blatant flattery, the sergeant managed to convince him that without the benefit of his advice, he would not know whether to keep the second murder quiet or not. The phone calls made, they both settled down to wait.

11

On Newton's instructions, Wainwright met the four men at the front entrance to the hospital, so that none of them would have the opportunity either of going to the psychological laboratory or finding out from the porter that the detective had been there within the preceding few minutes.

Standing at the door of the office, which Wainwright had left ajar, Newton could hear Poynter complaining about the lateness of the hour, the inconvenience of having to come at all and demanding to know what was going on. He quietly opened the door a little further and stood there for a moment surveying the scene.

'Good evening, gentlemen.'

Four pairs of eyes swivelled round and almost immediately, Poynter rose to his feet.

'Look here, Newton, we've all had a hard day at the hospital and you'd better not have brought us here for nothing.'

'I don't think you need worry yourself on that score, Dr Poynter.'

The detective threaded his way between the chairs and sat down next to Wainwright behind the desk. He looked steadily at each man in turn and then cleared his throat.

'One of you knows very well what has happened, but I will put the rest of you in the picture. Anne Wilkinson's death was not planned; one of the nurses fainted, the intended victim went to her aid and thus escaped the injection meant for her. Unfortunately the wretched girl didn't escape for long — she was found murdered yesterday morning.' He paused and looked round at all of them again. 'One of you killed them both.'

Renfrew took his pipe out of his mouth. 'I don't see how you can be so sure of that.'

'I wasn't, not until this evening. You will no doubt remember that I sent each of you an identical note during the committee meeting with a number written on it. I had two replies; one was from you, Renfrew, saying that you knew nothing about it and the other was an invitation to go to your laboratory, Leighton.'

'I never . . .' Leighton began, but Newton continued as if he had never been interrupted.

'When I got there, I was locked into one of the rooms and was very nearly killed by gas sent in through the ventilation system. Yes, I know it sounds melodramatic, but that's what happened. Now, only one of you four could have been responsible for that and the burning question is, which one? I think perhaps it would be fairest to start with the most junior.'

'Is it really necessary to go through this charade?'

Leighton started to get out of his chair, but Raymond, who was sitting next to him, put a restraining hand on his shoulder and muttered something to him in such a low voice that Newton was unable to pick it up.

'Now, Dr Leighton; you were involved in a complaint by one of the nurses during your psychological experiments and I did wonder about you for a time. We have reason to believe that the second victim was a blackmailer with a line in photography — one of the things you did was to have the nurses photographed in the nude, wasn't it?'

'This is outrageous, I'm . . . '

Newton totally ignored the interruption and pulled a piece of paper out of his pocket. 'I was inveigled into your laboratory this evening by this note and it happens to have your name on the bottom.'

'It's a forgery, I never . . . '

'I agree with you, but was it written by someone else, or did you do it, say with your left hand, in an attempt to make it look as if it came from someone else?'

Leighton seemed about to protest again, but then changed his mind and sat slumped in his chair, looking flushed and angry.

'By the way, I'm afraid I made rather a mess of your lab; I had to smash the two-way mirror and break the door down.' He shifted his gaze. 'Professor

Raymond.' The man took his cheroot out of his mouth and bowed ironically. 'Now you had the easiest access to the botulinus toxin. It is true that you might not have selected that method knowing that suspicion would have fallen on you, but, on the other hand, you might have thought you would have got away with it — for that matter if it hadn't been for the fact that Golding is a brilliant pathologist and was doing a special investigation on the 'flu victims, no one would have suspected that Anne Wilkinson's death was due to other than natural causes. You, of course, had the best opportunity of putting the poisoned syringe in position, but then you were also the one person amongst those of you here who would have seen exactly what was happening at the trolley. Would you have been callous enough to have allowed both the wrong and completely innocent girl to die a horrible death like that without stopping it, which you could easily have done without any risk to yourself? I doubt it. But then, of course I found this near those gas cylinders in Leighton's lab.' He opened the contents of the brown envelope on to the palm of his hand and held it out. 'I believe you always smoke these cheroots when you're nervous, don't you? Careless of you to have left it where it was bound to be found.'

Raymond drew on his cigar so that the tip glowed red. 'Very careless indeed, if I had done such a thing, which I didn't.'

'And you're not a careless man at all, are you? And I can't see even the most careless of medical men smoking in the same small room as a couple of cylinders of cyclopropane, not to mention the fact that the valves of both of them were open — I'm told that the gas is highly explosive.' Newton shifted his gaze in Renfrew's direction and the man altered his position and cleared his throat nervously. 'And what about the Colonel? The second victim died of curare poisoning and Golding has a theory that a quick acting anaesthetic was used beforehand. Curare, botulinus toxin, the skilful use of anaesthetics — you were a member of the British Army expedition to the Peruvian Andes, weren't you, and curare comes from South America, doesn't it? And anaesthetics were your speciality in the RAMC, weren't they? Would you have used those methods knowing that we would check your background? I wonder.' Newton turned towards Poynter, who was sitting hunched up in his chair. 'And finally we come to the senior physician, who also takes an interest in young nurses. Was it just your devotion to duty that kept you examining the new intakes for all those years and so thoroughly at that, more thoroughly in fact than at any other London teaching hospital?'

'Look here, Newton,' he said, his face purple with rage, 'if you think you can sit there making unpleasant insinuations about all of us with complete impunity, then you've got another think coming. I would remind you that there are witnesses to what you are saying.'

'In some ways,' Newton continued, completely unruffled, 'you seemed the most unlikely of the four, but then I argued that perhaps the various things that seemed to connect the others with the crimes might have been deliberately suggested by the one man who had no obvious connection with them at all.'

'I've warned you once; this time you've gone too far.'

'That might have been true if we hadn't found the girl this evening.'

'What girl?'

'How do you think we discovered the combination number of that safe so quickly? The murdered girl had a friend and not only did she tell us about the safe, but although she was reluctant at first, she decided to spill the rest of the beans.'

'This is preposterous. Do you really think anyone would believe that a man in my position would consort with common prostitutes?'

Newton felt like shouting aloud in triumph. 'Who,' he said with quiet emphasis, 'mentioned anything about prostitutes?'

Poynter suddenly seemed to have aged ten years, clutching at his chest and doubling up. 'Must take one of my tablets,' he muttered.

The physician reached into his jacket

pocket, took a white capsule from a small box and swallowed.

'Dr Poynter,' Newton began, 'I . . . '

The man held up his hand. 'You can spare me that. Caroline Ford deserved to die — she was nothing but a vicious blackmailer — but I grieved deeply about the other one; she was such a pretty girl.' He sighed deeply. 'I always did have a weakness for pretty girls; is that such a terrible crime?'

His breathing began to deepen and he passed a hand across his forehead, half rose from his chair and then fell back with a crash, his lips already turning blue. Raymond was there first, but by the time he had the physician on the ground and had started artificial respiration, the man was twitching all over and seconds later he was dead, the sickly smell of bitter almonds filling the room.

'Cyanide,' the pathologist said slowly and rose shakily to his feet.

There was a long silence, which was at last broken by Renfrew. 'I've got a bottle of whisky in my office, Newton,' he said, raising his eyebrows interrogatively.

'Good idea, I certainly owe you gentlemen an explanation. George, will you deal with everything here, please?'

Ten minutes later, they were sitting in Renfrew's office and the Colonel took a long drink from his glass.

'My God, that's better. I don't mind telling you, Newton, that that was the worst twenty minutes of my life and I've been in a few sticky corners in my time. Was it really necessary to put us through all that?'

'I'm afraid so. You see, although I knew that it had to be one of you, I had no hard evidence at all and my one hope was that in a confrontation, the guilty man would give himself away. He did, but only just; how Poynter managed to avoid reacting when what he fondly imagined to be a corpse, walked in, I can't imagine. I must say that when none of the rest of you did either, my confidence was shaken more than a little.'

'But what was that about the other girl you mentioned,' said Raymond.

'We'll probably never know all the details, but it seems clear to me now that

Poynter was a frequenter of prostitutes and was foolish enough to have had his photograph taken in compromising circumstances. Caroline Ford, the second girl to be murdered, was one of the nurses here and was in the same line of business. She either took the photo herself, or perhaps more likely, got hold of it from one of her colleagues and then tried to blackmail him. He obviously intended the botulinus toxin for her, but the fact of one of the nurses going into a faint altered the order in the queue and it was given to the wrong girl. With all that 'flu about, Caroline would never have suspected that Anne Wilkinson had been murdered; as it turned out, she was taken ill with the disease herself and Poynter must have gone to her flat and forced her to give him the number of the combination of her safe, no doubt removing the photograph before killing her, again using a method — Golding thinks it was curare — that might have been taken for the 'flu.

'While my assistant was searching her flat, her friend came in to see how she was and that's how we discovered the combination so quickly. Unfortunately she managed to get away while Sergeant Wainwright was looking through the safe. She would, of course, have been a key witness if only we had been able to hold on to her, particularly if she had seen the photograph — assuming always that I'm right in my theory about there being a photograph.'

'I think you can take it that there was one all right.'

They all looked round at Leighton, who up to that moment had hardly said a word. 'As you know, Newton, Poynter helped me out over that trouble I had with that psychological investigation on the nurses. Well, he wanted to see all the results I had obtained and when he returned the papers, several of the photographs were missing. I did think of tackling him about it, but I was anxious not to stir up any further trouble and so destroyed all the rest of them.'

'So you think that photographs of that type gave him a kick?'

'Yes, it certainly looks like it.'

'That seems pretty extraordinary to

me,' said Raymond, 'posed photographs showing absolutely everything are easy enough to obtain these days, even on book-stalls.'

'But not of girls he actually knew himself,' replied the detective, 'I would imagine that that was what he found exciting. It wouldn't surprise me if we found quite a collection when we come to search his place.'

'There's one thing that I don't understand,' said Raymond, 'and that's why he chose botulinus toxin in the first place. Of course I realize that as a murder weapon it was almost ideal, but he must have known that the girl had blackmail evidence hidden away somewhere and he would hardly have wanted to run the risk of it getting into the hands of the police.'

'I don't know that it would have been as risky as all that, particularly if her death had been put down to natural causes, which it certainly would have been if Golding hadn't been doing that special investigation. Prostitutes and blackmailers are not usually the sort of people who confide in bank managers or solicitors and even if she had left the evidence with someone like that, he would still probably have got away with it.'

'I've got another idea about that,' said Renfrew. 'I've seen someone with botulinus poisoning in South America and in many ways its effects are like those of curare. If Poynter managed to force the girl Caroline to give him the evidence under the latter drug, I imagine he was aiming to do the same with the botulin — it's a poison that takes some time to act and he was no doubt planning to follow her back to her flat after she had been injected. It's quite possible to keep people alive with artificial respiration under either of the two toxins and if you can imagine a more terrifying experience than that I can't. I know, I was once given a large dose of curare for experimental purposes without an anaesthetic when it was first introduced as a muscle relaxant and I still dream about it.'

'It's an extraordinary thing, isn't it,' said Raymond, 'one can work with a man for twenty years, play golf with him, confide in him and still not know him at all. Damn it, I liked the fellow and he was a very fine physician.'

Newton wasn't listening. Two young nurses had died, the senior physician of one of London's greatest hospitals had committed suicide and he had nearly been killed himself, but at that moment he wasn't thinking about all that; his thoughts were with the pathetic woman still in the sick bay and what the circumstances surrounding Poynter's death would do to her. That was the final obscenity in the whole sordid affair.

THE END